LEGACY OF
HIS REVENGE

LEGACY OF HIS REVENGE

CATHY WILLIAMS

MILLS & BOON

First published in Great Britain 2017
by Mills & Boon, an imprint of HarperCollins*Publishers*
1 London Bridge Street, London, SE1 9GF

Large Print edition 2018

© 2017 Cathy Williams

ISBN: 978-0-263-07356-0

MIX
Paper from
responsible sources
FSC® C007454

This book is produced from independently certified
FSC™ paper to ensure responsible forest management.
For more information visit www.harpercollins.co.uk/green.

Printed and bound in Great Britain
by CPI Group (UK) Ltd, Croydon, CR0 4YY

CHAPTER ONE

'THERE'S A DAUGHTER.'

In receipt of this revelation, Matias Rivero looked at his friend and trusted associate, Art Delgado. Like Matias, Art was thirty-two. They had gone to school together and had formed an unlikely friendship with Matias the protector, the one who always had his friend's back. Small, asthmatic and bespectacled, Art had always been an easy target for bullies until Matias had joined his class and, like a dangerous, cruising shark, had ensured that no one came near the boy who had spent the past two years dreading the daily onslaught of beatings.

Now, all these years later, Matias was Art's boss and in return Art was his most loyal employee. There was no one Matias trusted more. He motioned for Art to sit and leaned forward to take the mobile phone handed to him.

He scrolled down the three pictures capturing a small, homely, plump little creature leaving Carney's mansion in an old car that looked as though its only wish was to breathe its last breath and depart for the great automobile parking lot in the sky.

Matias vaguely wondered why she wasn't in a car befitting a man who had always made social climbing his priority.

But more than that he wondered who the hell the woman was and why he hadn't heard of her before.

'How is it that I am only now finding out that the man has a child?' Matias murmured, returning the mobile phone to his friend and relaxing back in the chair. 'In fact, how do you know for sure that the woman is his daughter?'

At a little after seven, his office was empty. It was still summertime hot, it was Friday and everyone else had better things to do than work. There was nothing pressing to hold his attention. His last lover had been dispatched a few weeks ago. Right now, Matias had all the time in the world to think about this development in his campaign.

'She said so,' Art told him, pushing his wire-rimmed spectacles up his nose and looking at his friend with some concern. 'But I don't suppose,' he added uneasily, 'it makes any difference, Matias. Does it?'

Matias pushed his chair back and stood up. Seated, he was formidable. Standing, he towered. He was six feet three of solid, packed muscle. Black-haired and black-eyed, the product of an Argentinian father and a dainty Irish mother, Matias had resoundingly come up trumps in the genetic lottery. He was sinfully beautiful, the hard lines of his lean face wonderfully chiselled into absolute perfection. Right at this moment, he was frowning thoughtfully as he strolled towards the floor-to-ceiling bank of glass that overlooked the busy London streets in the heart of the city.

From this high up, the figures down below were matchstick small and the cars and taxis resembled kids' toys.

He ignored the latter part of his friend's remark and instead asked, 'What do you mean "she said so"? Surely I would have known if the man had offspring. He was married and it was a childless union.' But in truth, Matias had been uninterested in the personal details of James Carney's life.

Why would he care one way or another if the man had kids or not?

For years, indeed for as long as he could remember, he had been focused on bringing the man to his knees through his company. The company that should never have been Carney's in the first place. The company that had been founded on lies, deceit and Carney's outright theft of Matias's father's invention.

Making money and having the power associated with it within his grasp was so entwined with his driving need to place himself in a position to reach out and wrench Carney's company from under his feet, that it would have been impossible to separate the two. Matias's march towards wealth had also been his march towards satisfying his thirst for revenge. He had gained his first-class degree, had bided his time in an investment bank for two years, making the money he needed to propel himself forward, and then he had quit with money under his belt and a black book stuffed with valuable connections. And he had begun his remorseless rise to the top via mergers and acquisitions of ailing companies, getting richer and richer and more and more powerful in the process.

Throughout it all, he had watched patiently for Carney's company to ail and so it had.

For the past few years, Matias had been circling the company, a predator waiting for exactly the right time. Should he begin the process of buying shares, then flooding the market with them so that he could plunge the company into a premature meltdown? Should he wait until the company's health deteriorated beyond repair so that he could instigate his hostile takeover? Choices, choices.

He had thought about revenge for so long that there was almost no hurry but the time had finally come. The letters he had recovered from his mother's possessions, before she had been admitted to hospital three weeks previously, had propelled him towards the inevitable.

'Well?' he prompted, returning to his chair although he was suddenly restless, itching now to start the process of retribution. 'You had a convivial conversation with the woman? Tell me how you came to your conclusion. I'm curious.'

Matias looked at Art, waiting for clarification.

'Pure coincidence,' Art admitted. 'I was about to turn into Carney's drive when she came speeding out, swerved round the corner, and banged into the car.'

'The woman crashed into my car? Which one?'

'The Maserati,' Art admitted. 'Nasty dent but her car, sadly, was more or less a write-off. No worries. It'll be sorted.'

'So she banged into my Maserati,' Matias hurried the story along, planning on returning to this little episode later down the line, 'told you who she was and then…what?'

'You sound suspicious, Matias, but that's exactly what happened. I asked her if that was the Carney residence and she said yes, that her dad lived there and she had just seen him. She was in a bit of a state because of the accident. She mentioned that he was in a foul mood and that it might be a good idea to rearrange whatever plans I had with him.'

'So there's a daughter,' Matias said thoughtfully. 'Interesting.'

'A nice girl, Matias, or so it would seem.'

'Impossible.' That single word was a flat denial. 'Carney is a nasty piece of work. It would be downright impossible for him to have sired anything remotely *nice*.' The harsh lines of his face softened. For all his friend's days of being bullied, Art had an instinctive trust in the goodness of human nature that he, Matias, lacked.

Matias had no idea why that was because they were both mixed race, in Art's case of Spanish descent on his mother's side. They had both started at the bottom of the pecking order and had had to toughen up to defend themselves against casual racism and snobbery.

But then, Matias mused not for the first time, he and he alone had witnessed first-hand the way criminal behaviour could affect the direction of someone's life. His father had met James

Carney at university. Tomas Rivero had been an extraordinarily clever man with a gift for all things mathematical. He had also been so lacking in business acumen that when, at the age of twenty-four, he invented a computer program that facilitated the analysis of experimental drugs, he was a sitting duck for a man who had very quickly seen where the program could be taken and the money that could be made out of it.

James Carney had been a rich, young thing with a tribe of followers and an eye to the main chance. He had befriended Tomas, persuaded him into a position of absolute trust and, when the time was right, had accumulated all the right signatures in all the right places that ensured that the royalties and dividends from the software went to him.

In return, Tomas had been sidelined with a third-rate job in a managerial position in the already ailing family business Carney had inherited from his father. He had never recovered mentally.

This was a story that had unfolded over the

years, although, in fairness to both his parents, nothing had ever been said with spite and certainly there had never been any talk of revenge on the part of either of them.

Matias's father had died over a decade previously and Rose Rivero, from the very start, had not countenanced thoughts of those wheels turning full circle.

What was done, was done, as far as she was concerned. The past was something to be relinquished.

Not so for Matias, who had seen his father in those quieter moments, seen the sadness that had become a humiliating burden. You didn't have to be a genius to work out that being shoved in some dingy back office while you saw money and glory heaped on undeserving shoulders had damaged his father irreparably.

As far as Matias was concerned, his father had never fully recovered from Carney's theft. He had worked at the company in the pitiful job condescendingly given to him for a couple of years and then moved on to another company, but by then his health was failing and Rose

Rivero had had to go out to work to help make ends meet.

If his mother had cautioned against revenge, then he had had enough of a taste for it for the both of them.

But he knew that over the years the fires had burned a little less brightly because he had become so intensely consumed in his own meteoric rise to the top. It had been propelled by his desire for revenge but along the way had gathered a momentum of its own, taken on its own vibrant life force…distracted him from the goal he had long ago set himself.

Until he had come upon those letters.

'She must have produced her insurance certificate,' Matias mused, eyes narrowing. 'What's the woman's name?'

'I'll email you the details.' Art sighed, knowing without having to be told the direction of his friend's thoughts. 'I haven't had a chance to look at it but I took a picture of the document.'

'Good,' Matias said with some satisfaction. 'Do that immediately, Art. And there will be no need for you to deal with this matter. I will handle it myself.'

'Why?' Art was the only person who would ever have dared ask such a forthright question. Especially when the question was framed in a tone of voice that carried a warning.

'Let's just say that I might want to get to know her better. Knowledge is power, Art, and I now regret that I didn't dig a little deeper into Carney's private life. But don't look so worried! I'm not the big bad wolf. I don't make a habit of eating innocent young girls. So if she's as *nice* as you imply, then she should be as safe as houses.'

'Your mother wouldn't like this,' Art warned bluntly.

'My mother is far too kind for her own good.' For a few seconds, Matias thought of Rose Rivero, who was recuperating from a near fatal stroke at one of the top hospitals in London. If his father had never recovered from Carney's treachery, then his mother had never recovered from his father's premature death. When you looked at it, Carney had not only been responsible for his family's unjust state of penury, but beyond that for the stress that had killed his father and for the ill health and unhappiness that had dogged his mother's life. Revenge had been a long time coming but, if only James Carney knew it, it was now a juggernaut rolling with unstoppable speed towards him…

Sophie Watts stared up at the soaring glass tower in front of her and visibly quailed.

The lovely man whose car she had accidentally *bruised* three days previously had been very accommodating when she had phoned the number he had given her when they had exchanged details. She had explained the situation with her insurance policy and he had been sympathetic. He had told her in a friendly enough voice that she would have to come and discuss the matter personally but he was sure that something could be sorted out.

Unfortunately, the building in front of her did not look like the sort of user-friendly place in which cheerful and accommodating people worked, sorting out thorny situations in a cordial and sympathetic manner.

She clutched her capacious bag tightly and continued staring. Her head told her that she had no option but to move forward with the crowd while her feet begged to be allowed to turn tail and flee back to her low-key corner of East London and her little house in which she did her small-scale catering and baking for anyone who needed her services.

She didn't belong here and the clothes she had carefully chosen to meet Art Delgado now felt ridiculous and out of place.

The young women sweeping past her with their leather computer bags and clicking high heels were all dressed in sharp black suits. They weren't dithering. They were striding with purpose into the aggressive glass tower.

A small, plump girl with flyaway hair wearing a summery flowered dress and sandals didn't belong here.

Sophie propelled herself forward, eyes firmly ahead. It had been a mistake to come here *first thing* so that she could *get it over with*. That idea had been great in theory but she hadn't banked on the early rush-hour stampede of city workers. However, it was too late now to start chastising herself.

Inside, the foyer was a wondrous and cruel blend of marble, glass and metal.

Arrangements of sofas were scattered here and there in circular formations. The sofas were all very attractive and looked enormously uncomfortable. Clearly management didn't want to encourage too much lounging around. Ahead of her, a bank of receptionists was busily directing people while streams of smartly dressed worker bees headed for the gleaming lifts opening and closing just beyond an array of stunted palm trees in huge ceramic pots.

Sophie felt a pang of physical longing for her kitchen, where she and Julie, her co-worker, chatted and baked and cooked and made big plans for the upmarket bakery they would jointly open one day. She craved the feel of her apron, the smell of freshly baked cake and the pleasant playing around of ideas for meals they had booked in for catering jobs. Even though she was now talking to one of the receptionists, explaining who she wanted to see, confirming that an appointment had been made and stuttering over her own name, she was unhappily longing to be somewhere else.

Frayed nerves made her miss what the snappily dressed girl in front of her had just said but then she blinked and registered that a mistake had been made.

'I don't know a Mr... River,' she said politely.

'Rivero.' Eyebrows arched up, lips tightened, eyes cooled.

'I'm here to see a Mr Delgado.'

'Your meeting is with Mr Rivero.' The receptionist swivelled the computer towards her. 'You are to sign in. Anywhere on the screen will do and just use your finger. Mr Rivero's secretary will be waiting for you on the tenth floor. Here's a clip-on pass. Make sure you don't remove it because if you do you'll be immediately escorted out of the building.'

In a fluster, Sophie did as she was told but her heart was hammering inside her as she obeyed instructions, allowing herself to be swept along in a group towards the nearest lift and then staring fixedly at nothing in particular as she was whooshed up to the tenth floor, as directed.

Who was Mr Rivero? She had banked on the comfort of explaining her awkward situation to the very nice Mr Delgado. What sort of hearing was she going to get from a complete stranger? She was as tense as a bow string when, disgorged into the plushest surroundings she had ever seen, she was taken in hand by a very tall, middle-aged woman whose expression of sympathy did nothing to quell her escalating nerves.

And then she was being shown into an office, faced with a closed door, ushered through it and deposited like an unwanted parcel in a room that was simply breathtaking.

For a few seconds, eyes as round as saucers, Sophie looked around her. She hadn't budged from where she had been placed just inside the door of a gigantic office. She cravenly recoiled from actually being bold enough to walk forward. Bag clutched tightly in front of her, she gradually became aware of the man sitting behind the desk. It was as if, suddenly, she focused, and on focusing felt the thudding impact of shock because the guy she was staring at was the most stunningly drop-dead gorgeous specimen she had ever seen in her entire life.

Her breathing slowed and even though she knew she was staring, she couldn't help herself. His hair was raven black, his eyes the colour of the darkest, richest chocolate, his features lovingly and perfectly chiselled. He oozed the sort of stupendous sex appeal that made heads swing round for a second and third look.

The silence stretched and stretched between them and then it dawned on her that she was making an absolute fool of herself.

'Miss Watts.' Matias was the first to speak. 'Do you intend to hover by the door for the duration of this meeting?' He didn't get up to shake her hand. He didn't smile. He did nothing to put her at ease. Instead he nodded at the chair in front of his desk. 'Sit down.'

Sophie shuffled forward, not knowing whether she was expected to shake his hand as a formality, but his expression was so forbidding that she decided against it and instead sank into the leather chair. She almost immediately leaned forward and rushed headlong into the little speech she had earlier rehearsed.

'I'm really sorry about the car, Mr...er... Rivero. I honestly had no idea that your friend was turning into the drive. It's so difficult to see round that bend, especially in summer. I admit I may have been driving a little faster than usual but I want to impress upon you that it was *unintentional*.' What she could have added but didn't was that her vision had been blurred because she had been doing her utmost not to cry after a stormy and upsetting meeting with James Carney.

Matias was watching her intently, his dark eyes narrowed on her flushed and surprisingly pretty face. He was a man who went for catwalk models, with long, angular bodies and striking, photogenic faces, yet there was something alluring about the woman sitting in front of him. Something about the softness of her face, the pale, vanilla shade of her unruly hair, the perfect clarity of her aquamarine eyes, held his attention and he could only assume that it was because of her connection to James Carney.

He hadn't known the woman existed but the minute he had found out he had recognised the gift that had landed in his lap for what it was.

He thought back to those letters he had unearthed, and his jaw tightened. That soft, wide-eyed, innocent look wasn't going to fool him. He didn't know the full story of the woman's relationship to Carney but he certainly intended to find out, just as he intended to exploit the situation he had been handed to discover if there were any other secrets the man might have been hiding. The broader the net was cast, the wider the catch.

'Employee,' Matias replied. This just in case she got it into her head that special favours were going to be granted because of Art's personal connection with him.

'I beg your pardon?'

'Art Delgado is my employee. He was driving my Maserati. Miss Watts, do you have any idea how much one costs?'

'No, I don't,' Sophie said faintly. He was having the most peculiar effect on her. It was as though the power of his presence had sucked the oxygen out of the air, making it difficult to breathe.

'In that case, allow me to enlighten you.' He named a sum that was sufficiently staggering to make her gasp. 'And I have been told that your insurance policy is invalid.'

'I didn't know,' Sophie whispered. 'I'm usually so good at dealing with all that stuff but things have been a bit hectic recently. I know I cancelled my old policy and I had planned on renewing with somewhere cheaper but…'

Matias held up one imperious hand to stop her in mid flow. 'I'm not interested in the back story,' he informed her coolly. 'To cut to the chase, the damage you have done to my car will run to many, many thousands.'

Sophie's mouth dropped open. 'Thousands?' she parroted.

'Literally. I'm afraid it won't be a simple case of sorting out the dent. The entire left wing of the car will have to be replaced. High-performance cars charge high-performance prices.'

'I... I had no idea. I haven't got that sort of money. I...when I spoke to your friend...sorry, your employee Mr Delgado on the phone, he said that we would be able to work something out.'

'Sadly working something out really isn't in his remit.' Matias thought that his old friend would raise a sardonic eyebrow at that sweeping statement.

'I could pay you back over time.' Sophie wondered what sort of time line would be acceptable to the unforgiving man staring coldly at her as though she were an undesirable alien that had suddenly invaded his personal space. She somehow didn't imagine that his time line was going to coincide with hers. 'I run a little catering business with a friend,' she hurtled on, desperate to bring this uncomfortable meeting to an end and even more desperate to find some sort of solution that wouldn't involve bankruptcy for her and Julie's fledgling start-up company. 'We only opened up a year and a half ago. Before that we were both primary school teachers. It's taken an awful lot of borrowing to get everything in order and to get my kitchen up to the required standard for producing food commercially, and right at this moment, well…there isn't a great deal of spare change flying about.'

'In other words you're broke.'

'We're really making a go of things, Mr Rivero!' Heat flared in her cheeks. 'And I'm sure we can work something out when it comes to a repayment schedule for your car…'

'I gather you're James Carney's daughter.' Matias lowered his eyes, then he pushed back his chair and stood up to stroll across to the impressive bank of windows, in front of which was a tidy sitting area complete with a low table fashioned in chrome and glass.

Sophie was riveted at the sight of him. The way he moved, the unconscious flex of muscle under the expensive suit, the lean length of his body, the casual strength he exuded that was frankly spellbinding. He turned to look at her and it took a big effort not to look away.

His throwaway remark had frozen her to the spot.

'Well?' Matias prodded. 'Art was on his way to pay a little visit to James Carney on business,' he expanded, 'when you came speeding out of his drive like a bat out of hell and crashed into my car. I had no idea that the man even had a family.' He was watching her very carefully as he spoke and was mildly surprised that she didn't see to ask him a very fundamental question, which was why the heck should Carney's private life have anything to do with him?

Whatever she was, she clearly didn't have a suspicious nature.

Sophie was lost for words. She had been shaken by the accident, upset after the visit to her father, and Art Delgado, so different from this flint-eyed guy assessing her, had encouraged her into a confidence she rarely shared with anyone.

'Of course...' Matias shrugged, curiosity spiking at her continued silence '... I am not primarily concerned with the man's private life but my understanding was that he was a widower.'

'He is,' Sophie whispered, ashamed all over again at a birthright she hadn't asked for, the consequences of which she had been forced, however, to live with.

'So tell me where you fit in,' Matias encouraged. 'Unless, of course, that was a little white lie you told my employee on the spur of the moment.' He appeared to give this a little thought. 'Maybe you were embarrassed to tell the truth…?'

'Sorry?' That garnered her attention and she looked at him with a puzzled frown.

'Young girl having an affair with an old man? I can see that you might have been embarrassed enough to have said the first thing that came to your head, anything that sounded a little less unsavoury than what you really are to Carney.'

'How dare you?' Sophie gasped, half standing. 'That's disgusting!'

'I'm just trying to do the maths.' Matias frowned and tilted his head to one side. 'If you're not his lover, the man must have had a mistress while he was married. Am I right? Are you Carney's love child?'

Sophie laughed bitterly because nothing could have been further from the truth. Love had never come into the equation. Before her untimely death, her mother, Angela Watts, had been an aspiring actress whose great misfortune had been her Marilyn Monroe blonde-bombshell looks. Prey to men's flattery and pursued for her body, she had made the fatal error of throwing her net too wide. James Carney, young, rich and arrogant, had met her at a club and, like all the others, had pursued her, but he had had no intention of ever settling down with someone he considered a two-bit tart with a pretty face. Those details had been drummed into Sophie from as soon as she was old enough to understand. He had had fun with Angela and she had foolishly thought that the fun would actually go somewhere, but even when she had contrived to trap him with a pregnancy he had stood firm, only later marrying a woman he considered of the right class and social position.

'He met my mother before he was married,' Sophie confessed, belatedly adding, 'not that it has anything to do with…well, *anything*. Mr Rivero, I would be more than happy for you to draw up a schedule for repayment. I will sign it right here and right now and you have my word that you will have every penny I owe you back. With interest if that's what you want.'

Matias burst out laughing. 'That's very obliging of you,' he drawled lazily. 'Believe it or not, I haven't become a successful businessman by putting my faith in the impossible. I have no idea what you owe the bank but I suspect you're probably barely making ends meet. Am I right?'

He tilted his head to one side and Sophie looked at him with loathing. He might be sinfully handsome but she had never met anyone she hated more on the spot. She wasn't stupid. He had all the money in the world, from the looks of it, but he wasn't going to be lenient when it came to getting back every penny she owed him and she knew that he wouldn't give a hoot if he drove her little company into the ground to do it.

Right now, he was toying with her like a cat playing with a mouse.

'We could work out a schedule,' he mused, 'but I would be on my walking frame before you made the final payment.' She really had the most wonderfully transparent face, he thought.

Impossible though it was, she looked as pure as the driven snow.

But perhaps she wasn't fashioned in the same mould as the father. Certainly, she wouldn't have had the example set by him on a daily basis if she was the product of a youthful affair. He was surprised, in fact, that she had any contact with the man at all and he wondered how that had worked when Carney's socially acceptable wife had been alive.

Matias wasn't going to waste time pondering stuff like that, however. Right now, he was working out how best to use her to his advantage. When he pulled the plug on Carney, he intended to hit him on all fronts and he wondered whether she could be of use to him in that.

What other secrets was the man hiding? Matias knew that the company was beset with financial problems but, in the ether, there had been rumours of foul play... Sometimes skeletons were hard to find, however hard you dug, and Carney was a man who was sly and smart enough to cover his tracks. Wouldn't it be satisfying if all his dark secrets were to be exposed to the cruel glare of light…?

Could this fresh-faced girl be the key to unlock more doors? And what if there were personal skeletons? An attack on all fronts was certainly worth considering. He was honest enough to acknowledge that this level of revenge was probably beneath him, but those letters he'd found… they had made this personal…

'You could always ask Daddy for the money,' he ventured smoothly, knowing what the answer would be.

'No!' This time she did stand up. Her full mouth was drawn into a thin, obstinate line. 'I won't have…my father involved in this. Bankrupt me if you want.' She reached into her bag, pulled out one of the business cards, remembering how filled with optimism she and Julie had been when they had had them printed. 'Here's my business card. You can come and see the premises. It's just in my kitchen but the equipment must be worth something. I have a number of big jobs lined up, so if you're patient I can do those and you can have the money. As for the rest... I will sell my house and I should be able to sort out the rest of the debt with money left over after the mortgage has been covered.'

Matias looked at her, every line of his powerful body indicating a man totally relaxed, totally unfazed by her emotional outburst.

Dark eyes roamed over her. She had tried to do something businesslike with her hair but somewhere along the line it had rebelled and tangled, white-blonde strands already curling around her cheeks. Her eyes were wide and a curious shade of turquoise and fringed, he noted, with thick dark lashes, which was at odds with the colour of her hair. And her body...

He shifted in his chair, astonished that he was even bothering to notice that she had curves in all the right places and luscious breasts that were prominent against the truly appalling flowered dress she was wearing.

She lacked sophistication and clearly had no style gene whatsoever, so what, he wondered, with a certain amount of irritation, was it about her that captured his attention so completely?

'You're overreacting,' he told her as she remained standing, her blue eyes dark with worry, anger and distress.

'You've just told me that you're not willing to come to any kind of arrangement with me about the money I owe you for your stupid car!' Easy-tempered by nature, Sophie was shocked at the stridency of her voice and the fact that she *was yelling at him*! 'I can't go to my bank and draw out the kind of money I would need to make good the damage. So, *of course I'm going to be upset.*'

'Sit down.'

'No. I'm going. You can get in touch with me on the number on the card! I'm going to have to talk this through with Julie. I don't know what she's going to say. She's put in most of her savings to try and get this business of ours going, as have I, so I'm going to have to find the money to pay her back too and make sure she doesn't have to pay for my mistake.' Her voice was wobbling and she stared off into the distance in an attempt to stop herself from crying.

Matias squashed all feelings of guilt. Why should he feel guilty? He was staring at a woman whose father had destroyed his family. In that scenario, guilt didn't exist. After all, all was fair in love and war, wasn't it?

'You could do that,' he murmured, 'or you could sit back down and listen to the proposition I have for you.'

CHAPTER TWO

'GO EASY ON THE GIRL,' Art had urged his friend the previous day. 'Because Carney's her father, doesn't mean that she has been cut from the same cloth.'

Matias hadn't argued the point with his friend, but he had privately held the view that the apple never fell far from the tree and an innocent smile and fluttering eyelashes, which he was guessing had been the stunt the woman had pulled on Art, didn't mean she had a pure soul.

Now, however, he was questioning the judgement call he had made before he had even met her. He was seldom, if ever, wrong when it came to summing people up, but in this instance his friend might have had a point. Matias wasn't going to concede that the woman spent all her spare time helping the poor and unfortunate or that she was the sort who wouldn't have recognised an uncharitable thought if it did a salsa in front of her. What he *did* recognise was that he would be better served in his quest for revenge by getting to know her.

She was an unexpected piece of a puzzle he had thought was already complete and he would have to check her out.

He had waited years for retribution. Waiting a couple of weeks longer wasn't going to kill him and it might put him in an even stronger position than he already was.

He looked at her anxious face and smiled slowly. 'There's no need to look so worried,' he soothed. 'I'm not a man who beats about the bush, Miss…it *is* Miss, isn't it?'

Sophie nodded and automatically touched her ring-free finger. Once upon a time, she had had a boyfriend. Once upon a time, she had had dreams of marriage and kids and a happy-ever-after life, but reality had had something different to say about that.

'Boyfriend?' Matias hadn't missed that unconscious gesture. No ring on her finger. Had there been one? Once? Was she divorced? She looked far too young, but who knew? It wasn't his business but it paid to know your quarry.

Sophie sat on her hands. 'I don't see what that has to do with…your car, Mr…Rivers…'

'Rivero.' Matias frowned because it wasn't often that anyone forgot his name. In fact, never. 'And in point of fact, it has. You owe me money but if you're telling the truth, then it would seem that you have little to no hope of repaying me.'

'Why wouldn't I be telling the truth?'

Matias debated whether he should point out that her father would surely not be keen to see his child slaving in front of a hot oven cooking food for other people, so how likely was it that catering was her full-time occupation? Or maybe she was the sort who rebelled against their parents by pretending to reject money and everything it stood for? When you came from money and had comfort and security as a blanket to fall back on, it was easy to play at enjoying poverty. From what he knew of the man, keeping up appearances ran to a full-time occupation and surely his offspring would have been dragged into that little game too?

However, he had no intention of laying any of his cards on any tables any time soon. At any rate, it would be a matter of seconds to check her story and he was pretty sure she was telling the truth. Her car, for one thing, did not suggest someone with an enviable bank balance and the oversight with the insurance added to the impression.

He shrugged. 'Maybe you imagine that pleading poverty will touch some kind of chord in me.'

'That never crossed my mind,' Sophie said honestly. 'I can't think that anyone would be mad enough to try and appeal to your better nature.'

'Come again?' Momentarily distracted, Matias stared at her with outright incredulity.

The woman was here on the back foot, staring bankruptcy in the face if he decided to go after her, and yet she had the cheek to *criticise him*? He almost couldn't believe his ears.

Sophie didn't back down. She loathed arguments and avoided confrontation like the plague, but she was honest and forthright and could be as stubborn as a mule. She had had to be because she had had to take up where her mother had left off when it came to breathing in deep and pursuing what she felt James Carney owed her.

Right now, she had no idea where Matias was going with some of his remarks. He had mentioned a solution to the problem staring her in the face, but she couldn't help noticing that he hadn't actually said what that solution might be.

If he was stringing her along only to pull the rug from under her feet, then she wasn't going to sit back and allow him to bully her in the process.

'If you had a better nature,' she pointed out, 'then you would try and understand what it's like for me. You probably don't have a clue about what it's like to struggle, because if you did then you would be able to put yourself in my shoes, and if you did that you might try and find a solution to the problem instead. If you give me a chance, then I will pay you back, but first you have to give me a chance.'

'Is this your idea of buttering me up?' Matias said coldly. 'Because if it is, then you're heading in the wrong direction. Let's not forget that you're here with a begging bowl.' He would come back to her father and exactly how hard he'd made Matias's family *struggle* in due course.

Sophie's soft mouth tightened. She had a lot of experience when it came to begging bowls and she had learned the hard way that buckling under threat never got anyone anywhere.

'You said that you had a proposition for me,' she reminded him, clinging to that lifebelt and already willing to snatch at it whatever the cost. Perhaps if she had had only herself to think about, she might have backed off, but there were more people at stake here than just her.

Matias was already pleased that he had decided to go with the flow and exploit the opportunity presented to him. Soft and yielding she might look, but it had quickly become apparent that she was anything but.

He felt the kick of an unexpected challenge. So much of his life was predictable. He had reached the pinnacle of his success and he was still in his early thirties. People kowtowed to him, sought his advice, hung onto his every word, did their utmost to please him. Bearing in mind that financial security and the power that came with it had been his ambition for as long as he could remember, he was now disappointed to acknowledge that there was something missing from his life, something that not even the glowing fires of revenge had been able to fulfil.

He had become jaded over time. When he thought back to the hungry young man he had once been, his whole body alive for the task he had set himself, he felt as if he were staring backwards at a stranger. Certainly, on a personal level, the fact that he could have any woman he wanted was something that had long lost its novelty value. Now, for the first time in ages, he was facing a challenge he could sink his teeth into and he liked the feeling.

'In two weeks' time...' Matias had returned to his desk and now he pushed back his leather chair and relaxed with his hands folded behind his head '... I am due to host a long weekend party at one of my houses. Around eighty people will be descending and they will be expecting

the highest standard of catering. I will provide
the food. You will handle everything else. Naturally, you won't be paid. Succeed and we can
carry on from there. I have no intention of exer-
cising my right to frankly bankrupt you because,
for a start, driving without being insured is ille-
gal. If I went the whole way, you'd be in prison
by dusk. Instead, I will play it by ear.'

'In other words,' Sophie said stiffly, 'you'll
own me until you consider the debt to be paid
off.'

Matias tilted his head to one side and smiled
coolly. 'That's one way of putting it...' Okay, so
it was the only way of putting it. He would be
able to take his time finding out about her and
thereby finding other ways back to her father.
Were those rumours of foul play in the company
vaults true? Was that something the man had
confessed to his offspring? If so, if that level of
information could somehow be accessed, then
he would have the most powerful weapon for
revenge within his grasp. He couldn't care less
about the damage to his car. He could take it
to the nearest scrapyard and buy a replacement

without even noticing any dent in his limitless income.

'And when you think about the alternatives,' he mused, 'you'll conclude, pretty fast, that it's a sweet deal for you.' He gave a gesture that was as exotically foreign as he was. 'You might even be able to…' he flicked out the business card she had earlier given him '…distribute these discreetly during the weekend.'

'And will I be able to bring my business partner?'

'I don't think so. Too many cooks and all that. I will ensure that you have sufficient staff to help but essentially this will be your baby.' He glanced at his watch but didn't stand, leaving it to Sophie to deduce that he was done with her. She stood up awkwardly and looked at him.

How could someone so effortlessly beautiful be so utterly cold-hearted?

Although, she had to acknowledge, at least he hadn't done what he had every right to do and contacted the police. She could have kicked herself for that little window during which she had forgotten to renew her insurance with a different company. So unlike her but then she had had so much on her mind.

'Will there be something…er…in writing?'

'Something in writing?'

'Just so that I know how much of the debt will be covered when I handle the catering for you that weekend…'

'You don't trust me?'

Sophie gazed off and thought of her father. She'd had to learn fast how to manage him. Trust had never been in plentiful supply in their relationship and she thought that it would be prudent not to rely on it in this situation either.

'I don't trust many people,' she said quietly and Matias's ears pricked up.

He looked at her carefully. 'No?' he murmured. 'I don't trust many people either but then, as you've pointed out, I don't have a better nature whereas I expect you probably do. Am I right?'

'I've found that people inevitably let you down,' Sophie told him painfully, then she blinked and wondered what on earth had induced her to say that. 'So it would work if I could have something in writing as I go along…'

'I'll get my secretary to draw something up.' All business now, Matias stood up, signalling that her time was up. 'Rest assured, you won't be required to become my personal slave in return for a debt.'

His dark eyes flicked to her as she shuffled to her feet. She gave the impression of someone whose eyes were always downcast and he could see how Art had been knocked sideways by her meek persona, but he wasn't so easily fooled. He had seen the fire burning just below the surface. She blushed like a virgin but those aquamarine eyes flashed like a siren call and he couldn't wait to get to the bottom of her...and discover in the process what she could contribute to the picture he had already compiled of her father.

'But I just think that there must have been *some other way* of sorting this situation out! I'm going to be left here for *several days* on my own and I just don't know whether I can manage the Rosses' cocktail party on my own!'

Sophie's heart went out to Julie and she looked at her friend sympathetically. Sympathy was about all she could offer. She had signed up to a deal with the devil and it was a better deal than she might have hoped for. Even though she hated it.

She had been over all the pros and cons of the situation, and had apologised profusely to her friend, who was not as confident in the kitchen as she was.

'But on the bright side,' she said in an upbeat voice, 'think of all the possible connections we could make! And,' she felt compelled to repeat because fair was fair, 'he could have just taken everything from us to sort out the damage to his car. I honestly had no idea *that a car* could cost that much to repair! It's mad.'

He was sending a car for her and Sophie looked at her watch with a sense of impending doom. A fortnight ago, his secretary had emailed her with an extensive list of things she 'should bring, should know and should be prepared to undertake'.

There was to be no veering off from the menu and she would have to ensure that every single dish for every single day was prepared to the highest possible specification.

She was told how many helpers she would have and how they should behave. Reading between the lines, that meant *no fraternising with the guests*.

She was informed of the dress code for all members of staff, including herself. The dress code did not include jeans or anything that might be interpreted as casual.

She gathered that she was being thrown in at the deep end and this detailed information was his way of being kind to her. She assumed that he had diverted his original catering firm to some other do specifically so that he could put her through her paces and she had spent the past two nights worrying about what would happen if she failed. Matias Rivero wasn't, she thought, callous enough to take the shirt off her back, but he intended to get his money's worth by hook or by crook. He might be unwilling to throw her to the sharks, but he wasn't going to let her get off lightly by agreeing to monthly payments that would take her decades to deliver what was owed.

This was the biggest and most high-profile job she had ever got close to doing and the fact that he would be looking at her efforts with a view to criticism filled her with terror. She wondered whether he hadn't set her an impossible task just so he could do his worst with a clear conscience when she failed. He struck her as the sort of man who saw ruthlessness as a virtue.

His car arrived just as she was giving some final tips to Julie about the catering job she would be handling on her own, and Sophie took a deep breath and reached for her pull-along case.

There would be a uniform waiting for her at his country house, which was in the Lake District. However, his instructions had been so detailed that she had decided against wearing her usual garb of jeans and a tee shirt to travel there and, instead, was in an uncomfortable grey skirt and a white blouse with a short linen jacket. At a little after ten in the morning, with the sun

climbing in the sky, the outfit was already making her perspire.

She hung onto the hopeful thought that she
would probably find herself stuck in the kitchen
for the entire time. With any luck, she wouldn't
glimpse Matias or any of his guests and she
knew that, if that were the case, then she would
be all right because she was an excellent chef
and more than capable of producing the menu
that had been emailed to her.

She wouldn't even have to bother about sourc-
ing the ingredients, because all of that would already have been taken care of.

Her high hopes lasted for as long as the very
smooth car journey took. Then nerves kicked
in with a vengeance as the car turned between
imposing wrought-iron gates to glide sound-
lessly up a tree-lined avenue on either side of
which perfectly manicured lawns stretched towards distant horizons of open fields, shaded
with copses. It was a lush landscape and very
secluded.

The house that eventually climbed into view
was perched atop a hill. She had expected some-

thing traditional, perhaps a Victorian manor house with faded red brick and chimneys.

She gasped at the modern marvel that greeted her. The architect had designed the house to be an organic extension of the hill and it appeared to be embedded into the side so that glass and lead projected as naturally from rock and foliage as a tree might grow upwards from the ground.

The drive curved around the back, skirting a small lake, and then they were approaching the house from the side where a sprawling courtyard was large enough to house all those important guests she had been expecting to find. Except the courtyard was empty aside from three high-performance cars parked haphazardly.

All at once, a quiver of nervous tension rippled through her. She could have become lost in a crowd of people. In an empty mansion, and it certainly looked empty, getting lost wasn't going to be that easy.

And for reasons she couldn't quite understand, reasons that extended well beyond the uncomfortable circumstances that surrounded her presence here, Matias made her feel…awkward. Too *aware of herself,* uncomfortable in her own skin and on edge in a way she had never felt before.

Her bag was whipped away from her before she had time to offer to take it herself and then she was being led through a most marvellous building towards the kitchen by a soft-spoken middle-aged woman who introduced herself as Debbie.

It was a cavernous space of pale marble and pale walls on which were hung vast abstract canvasses. She could have been walking through the centre of a fabulous ice castle and she actually shivered because never had she felt so removed from her comfort zone.

It had been hot outside but in here it was cool and quite silent. When she finally turned her attention away from her impressive surroundings, it was to find that Debbie had disappeared and instead Matias was lounging in the doorway of the kitchen.

'You're here,' he commented, taking in the prissy outfit and the flat black pumps and the neat handbag, which had apparently replaced the Santa's sack she had been carrying the last time he had seen her. He straightened and headed straight back in the direction of the kitchen, expecting her to follow him, which she did.

Sophie was tempted to retort where else would she be when she'd had no choice, but instead, she said politely to his back, 'I expected it to have been a bit busier.'

'The first of the guests don't arrive until tomorrow.' Matias didn't bother to turn around. 'I thought you might find it helpful to acquaint yourself with the kitchen, get to know where everything is.'

They had ended up in a kitchen that was the size of a football field and equipped to the highest possible standard. Sophie felt her fingers itch as she stared around her, dumbstruck.

'Wow.' She turned a full circle, eyes as wide as saucers, then when she was once again looking at him, she asked, 'So are you going to show me where everything is?'

Matias looked blankly around him and Sophie's eyebrows shot up.

'You don't know your way around this kitchen at all, do you?'

'I'm not a cook so it's true to say that I've never had much time for kitchens. I'm seldom in one place for very long and I tend to eat out a great deal. I'm a great believer in the theory that if someone else can do something better than you, then it would be cruel to deny them the opportunity.'

Sophie laughed and was surprised that he had managed to make her laugh at all. Her cheeks warmed and she looked away from those piercing dark eyes. Her heart was beating fast and she was confused because once again she could feel the pull of an attraction that went totally against the grain.

For starters, he had proven himself to have all the characteristics she despised in a man. He was arrogant, he was ruthless and he had the sort of self-assurance that came from knowing that he could do what he wanted and no one would object. He had power, he had money and he had looks and those added up to a killer combination that might have been a turn-on for other women but was a complete turn-off for her.

She knew that because he was just an extreme

version of the type of men her mother had always been attracted to. Like a moth to an open flame, Angela Watts had been drawn to rich, good-looking men who had always been very, very bad for her. She had had the misfortune to have collided with the pinnacle of unsuitable men in James Carney, but even when that relationship had died a death she had still continued to be pointlessly drawn to self-serving, vain and inappropriate guys who had been happy to take her for a ride and then ditch her when she started to bore them.

Sophie had loved her mother but she had recognised her failings long before she had hit her formative teens. She had sworn to herself that, when it came to men, she would make informed choices and not be guided into falling for the wrong type. She would not be like her mother.

It helped that, as far as Sophie was concerned, she lacked her mother's dramatic bleached-blonde sex appeal.

And if she had made a mistake with Alan, then it hadn't been because she had chosen someone out of her league. It had just been…one of those things, a learning curve.

So why was she finding it so hard to tear her eyes away from Matias? Why was she so aware of him here in the kitchen with her, lean, indolent and darkly, dangerously sexy?

'Why don't you look around?' he encouraged, sitting at the kitchen table, content to watch her while he worked out how he was going to engineer the conversation into waters he wanted to explore.

She was very watchable. Even in clothes that were better suited to a shop assistant in a cheap retail outlet.

He was struck again by how little sense that made considering who her father was, but he would find out in due course and in the meanwhile…

He looked at her with lazy male appreciation. She had curves in all the right places. The hazy picture he had seen on Art's phone had not done justice to her at all. His eyes drifted a little south of her face to her breasts pushing against the buttons of the prissy, short-sleeved shirt. At least the jacket had come off. She was reaching up to one of the cupboards, checking the supply of dishes, he presumed, and the shirt ruched up to reveal a sliver of pale, smooth skin at her waist, and a dormant libido that should have had better things to do than start wanting to play with a woman who was firmly off the cards kicked into gear.

'Everything looks brand new.' Sophie turned to him, still on tiptoes, and he could see that indeed the crockery and the glasses in the cupboards could have come straight out of their expensive packaging. 'How often has this kitchen been used?'

'Not often,' Matias admitted, adjusting position to control his insurgent body. He glanced away for a few moments and was more in charge of his responses when he looked at her once more. Her hair was extraordinarily fair and he could tell it was naturally so. Fine and flyaway—with her heart-shaped face it gave her the look of an angel. A sexy little angel.

'In summer, I try and get up here for a weekend or so, but it's not often possible. Taking time out isn't always a viable option for me.'

'Because you're a workaholic?' Not looking at him, Sophie stooped down to expertly assess what the situation was with pots and pans and, as expected, there was no lack of every possible cooking utensil she might need. Next, she would examine the contents of the fridge.

With her catering hat firmly in place, it was easy to forget Matias's presence on the kitchen chair and the dark eyes lazily following her as she moved about the kitchen.

'I've discovered that work is the one thing in life on which you can depend,' Matias said, somewhat to his astonishment. 'Which, incidentally, is how I know your father.'

Sophie stilled and turned slowly round to look at him. 'You know my father? You actually *know* him?'

'I know *of* him,' Matias admitted, his dark eyes veiled. 'I can't say I've ever met the man personally. In fact, I was contemplating a business venture with him, which accounts for Art heading towards the house when you came racing out of the drive and crashed into my Maserati.' The delicate bones of her face were taut with tension and his curiosity spiked a little more.

'You had an appointment with my father?'

'Not as such,' Matias told her smoothly. 'Art was going to…let's just say…lay the groundwork for future trade…' In other words, he had sent Art to do the preliminary work of letting Carney know that his time was drawing to a close. He, Matias, would step in only when the net was ready to be tightened.

'Poor Art,' Sophie sighed, and Matias looked at her with a frown.

'Why do you say that?'

'I don't think he would have got very far with James even if he'd managed to gain entry to the house.'

'*James?* You call your father *James*?'

'He prefers that to being called Dad.' Sophie blushed. 'I think he thinks that the word *dad* is a little ageing. Also…'

'Also,' Matias intuited, 'you were an illegitimate child, weren't you? I expect he was not in the sort of zone where he would have been comfortable playing happy families with you and your mother. Not with a legitimate wife on the scene.'

Sophie went redder. What to say and how much? He was being perfectly polite. He wasn't to know the sort of man her father was and, more importantly, the reasons that had driven her mother to maintain contact with him, a legacy she had passed on to her daughter. Nor was she going to fill him in on her private business.

But the lengthening silence stretched her nerves to breaking point, and eventually she offered, reluctantly, 'No. My mother was a youthful indiscretion and he didn't like to be reminded of it.'

'He got your mother pregnant and he refused to marry her...' Matias encouraged.

Sophie stiffened because she could see the man in front of her was busy building a picture in his head, a picture that was spot on, but should she allow him to complete that picture?

The conversation she had had with her father just before she had blindly ended up crashing into Matias's car had been a disturbing one. He was broke, he had told her.

'And don't stand there with your hand stretched out staring gormlessly at me!' he had roared, pacing the magnificent but dated living room that was dark and claustrophobic and never failed to make Sophie shudder. 'You can take some of the blame for that! Showing up here month in month out with bills to settle! Now, there's *nothing left*. Do you understand me? *Nothing!*'

Cringing back against the stone mantelpiece, truly fearful that he would physically lash out at her, Sophie had said nothing. Instead, she had listened to him rant and rave and threaten and had finally left the house with far less than she had needed.

What if he was telling the truth? What if he *was* going broke? Where would that leave her...? *And more importantly, where would that leave Eric?*

As always, thinking of her brother made her heart constrict. For all her faults and her foolish misjudgements, her mother had been fiercely protective of her damaged son and had determined from early on that she wasn't going to be fobbed off by a man who had been happy enough to sleep with her for four years before abandoning her as soon as the right woman had finally appeared on the scene. She had used the only tool in her armoury to get the money she had needed for Eric to be looked after in the very expensive home where his needs were catered for.

Blackmail.

How would those fancy people James mixed with like him if they knew that he refused to support his disabled son and the family he had carelessly conceived, thinking that they would all do him a favour and vanish when it suited him?

James had paid up and he had continued paying up because he valued the opinion of other people more than anything else in the world, not because he felt any affection for either the son he had never seen or the daughter he loathed because she was just an extension of the woman who, as far as he was concerned, had helped send him to the poorhouse.

If there was no money left, Eric would be the one to pay the ultimate price and Sophie refused to let that happen.

If Matias was interested in doing a deal with her father, a deal that might actually get him solvent once again, then how could it be in her interests to scupper that by letting him know just how awful James was? If her father had money then Eric would be safe.

'That's life.' She shrugged, masking her expression. 'There aren't many men who would have found it easy to introduce an outside family to their current one.' She took a deep breath and said, playing with the truth like modelling clay, 'But he's always been there for my mother... And now...er...for me...financially...'

Matias wondered whether they were talking about the same person. 'So you would recommend him as someone I should have dealings with?'

Fingers crossed behind her back, Sophie thought of her brother, lost in his world in the home where she visited him at least once a week, her brother who would certainly find life very,

very different without all that care provided, care that only money could buy. 'Yes. Of course. Of course, I would.' She forced a smile. 'I'm sure he would love to have you contact him…'

CHAPTER THREE

MATIAS LOWERED HIS stunning dark eyes. So she either had no idea what kind of man her father was or she knew perfectly well enough and was tainted with the very same streak of greed, hence her enthusiasm for him to plough money into the man.

He wondered whether, over time and with her father's finances going down the drain faster than water running down a plughole, she had found herself an accidental victim of his limited resources. She had just declared that her father had supported her and her mother and Matias had struggled to contain a roar of derisive laughter at that. But she could have been telling the truth. Perhaps the dilapidated car and the debt owed to the bank were the result of diminishing handouts. She might have been an illegitimate child but it was possible that Carney had privately doted on her, bearing in mind that his own marriage had failed to yield any issue. Advertising a child outside marriage might have been no big deal for many men, but a man like Carney would have been too conscious of his social standing to have been comfortable acknowledging her publicly.

For a moment and just a moment, he wondered whether he could notch up some extra retribution and publicly shame the man by exposing a hidden illegitimate child, but he almost immediately dismissed it because it was…somehow unsavoury. Especially, he thought, shielding the expression in his dark eyes, when the woman sitting in front of him emanated innocence in waves. There was such a thing as a plan backfiring and, were a picture of her to be printed in any halfway decent rag, a sympathetic public would surely take one look at that disingenuous, sensationally sincere face and cast *him* in the role of the bad guy. Besides, Carney's close friends doubtless knew of the woman's existence already.

'I will certainly think about contacting your

father,' Matias intoned smoothly, watching her like a hawk. He became more and more convinced that she was playing him for a sap because she was suddenly finding it seemingly impossible to meet his eyes. 'Now, you've looked at the menu. Tell me whether you think you're up to handling it.'

Sophie breathed a sigh of relief at the change of subject. She hated the little white lie she had told, even though she was surely justified in telling it. Matias might be disgustingly rich and arrogant but he still didn't deserve to be deceived into believing her father was an honourable guy. On the other hand, if the choice was between her brother's future safety and well-being and Matias investing some money he wouldn't ever miss, then her brother was going to win hands down every time.

But that didn't mean that she'd liked telling Matias that fib.

She jumped onto the change of topic with alacrity. 'Absolutely.' She looked around her at the expensive gadgets, the speckled white counters, the vast cooking range. 'And it helps that your kitchen is so well equipped. Did you plan on doing lots of entertaining here when you bought the house?'

'Actually, I didn't buy the house. I had it built for me.' He went to the fridge, extracted a bottle of chilled white wine and poured her a glass. It seemed wildly extravagant to be consuming alcohol at this hour of the afternoon but she needed to steady her nerves, which were all over the place. 'And I had no particular plans to use the space for entertaining. I simply happen to enjoy having a lot of open space around me.'

'Lucky you,' Sophie sighed. After two sips of wine, she was already feeling a little less strung out. 'Julie and I would have a field day if we had this sort of kitchen. I've done the best with what I've got, but getting all the right equipment to fit into my kitchen has been a squeeze and if the business really takes off, then we're definitely going to have to move to bigger premises.'

Matias wondered whether that was why she had encouraged him to contact her father and put some work his way. Was it because she would be the happy beneficiary of such an arrangement?

Suspicious by nature and always alert to the threat of someone trying it on, he found it very easy to assume the worst of her, in defiance of the disingenuous manner she had. Judge a book by its cover and you almost always ended up being taken for a ride.

Not only did he have the example of his father to go on, who had paid the ultimate price for judging a book by its cover, but he, Matias, had made one and only one catastrophic misjudgement in his heady youth. On the road to the vast riches that would later be his and caught up in the novel situation of being sought after by men far older than himself who wanted to tap his financial acumen, he had fallen for a girl who had seemed to be grounded in the sort of normality he had fast been leaving behind. Next to the savvy beauties who had begun forming a queue for him, she had seemed the epitome of innocence. She had turned down presents, encouraged him to sideline the sort of fancy venues that were opening up on his horizon and professed a burning desire to go to the movies and share a bag of popcorn. No boring Michelin restaurants for her!

She had played the long game and he had been thoroughly taken in until she had sprung a pregnancy scare on him. Talk had turned to marriage pretty quickly after that and God knew he might just have ended up making the biggest mistake of his life and tying the knot had he not discovered the half-used packet of contraceptive pills in her handbag. Quite by accident. Only then, when he had confronted her, had her true colours emerged.

That narrow escape had been a turning point for him. A momentary lapse, he had discovered, was all it took for your life to derail. Momentary lapses would never again occur and they hadn't. Matias ruled his own life with a rod of steel and emotions were never allowed free rein. He took what he needed out of life and discarded what ceased to be of use to him.

Art was the only person on earth who knew about that brief but shameful episode and so it would remain. Matias had had little time for the perils of emotional roller-coaster rides, having grown up as witness to the way his father's emotional and trusting nature had led him down a blind alley, and his disastrous love affair had been the final nail in the coffin, after which he had entombed his heart in ice and that was exactly the way he liked it.

'You said you've only been in the catering business for a year and a half. What prompted the change of career?'

'We both enjoyed cooking.' Sophie realised that her glass of wine was empty and he appeared to have topped it up. She moved to sit at the wonderful kitchen table fashioned from black granite and metal. 'We became accustomed to friends asking us to cater for them and bit by bit we came to the conclusion that, in the long run, we might very well be better off doing something we both loved and were good at. Julie was fed up with her teaching job and I guess I just wanted a change of career.'

'It must have been a leap of faith for you. Changing career that dramatically takes guts.' Had she embarked on that career change with the mistaken impression that her father was still wealthy enough to fund her? Had she had to resort to borrowing from the bank when she found herself out of a job and unable to turn to her parent for a handout? Was that why she was struggling financially?

Lucas knew that James Carney's financial position had been poor for a few years.

'Maybe. Haven't *you* ever had to change career or were you born with a silver spoon in your mouth?' she asked.

'You say that as though you're not familiar with that situation yourself.'

'I'm not,' Sophie said flatly and Matias looked at her through narrowed eyes.

'I confess I find that hard to believe, given your father's elevated lifestyle.'

'I'd really rather not talk about him,' Sophie hedged warily.

'You don't like talking about your father? Why is that? I grant you, it must have been a nuisance living in the shadows, if indeed that was the case, but surely if, as you say, he helped you and your mother through the years…well, he must be quite a character because many men in a similar situation would have walked away from their responsibility.'

Sophie muttered something inaudible that might have been agreement or dissent.

'Of course, life must be altogether easier for you now,' Matias continued conversationally. 'I gather his wife died some years ago, so presumably he has taken you under his wing...'

'We don't have that sort of relationship,' Sophie admitted stiffly and Matias's ears pricked up.

'No?' he encouraged. 'Tell me about him. The reason I ask is simple. If I'm to have any financial dealings with him, it would be useful to try and understand the sort of person he is.'

'Do you take this close an interest in *all* your... er...clients?' This more to divert the conversation than anything else. Sophie had no real idea how people in the business world operated.

'I have slightly more elaborate plans for your father's company,' which wasn't exactly a lie, then he shrugged.

'Is that what you do?'

Matias frowned. 'Explain.'

'Well, do you…er…invest in companies? The truth is I honestly don't know the ins and outs of how companies operate. I've never had much interest in that sort of thing.'

'I see…so you don't care about money…'

'Not enough to have gone into a career where I might have made a fortune. Life would have been a lot easier if I had.' For starters, she thought, she wouldn't have had to endure the monthly humiliation of picking up where her mother had left off, and going to her father with cap in hand because Eric's home was costly and there was no other choice. 'I don't suppose I'm ruthless enough.'

'Is that a criticism of me?' Matias asked wryly, amused because it was rare for anyone to venture any opinion in his presence that might have been interpreted as critical. But then, as she had pointed out, whatever better nature he had was seldom in evidence and things weren't going to change on that front any time soon.

Sophie was caught between being truthful and toeing the diplomatic line. Talking about her father was out of bounds because sooner or later she would trip up and reveal exactly the sort of man he was. Telling Matias Rivero what she thought of him was also pretty questionable because he had thrown her a lifeline and he could whip it back whenever it suited him. If she succeeded in this task, a good proportion of her debt to him would be wiped out. As agreed, she had received a detailed financial breakdown of what she could expect from her weekend's work.

Getting on the wrong side of him wasn't a good idea. But he *had* asked…

And something about the man seemed to get her firing on cylinders she didn't know she possessed.

'Well, I *am* here,' she pointed out and Matias frowned.

'Where are you going with that?'

'You intend to get your pound of flesh from me by whatever means necessary and if that's not ruthless, then I don't know what is.'

'It's not ruthless,' Matias informed her, without a hint of an apology. 'It's good, old-fashioned business sense.' On more levels than she could ever begin to suspect, he thought, dispelling a fleeting twinge of guilt because all that mattered was getting her despicable father to pay for what he had done all those years ago.

Matias thought back to the slim stash of letters he had found shoved at the back of his mother's chest of drawers. He would never have come across those letters if she hadn't been rushed to hospital, because he had had to pack a bag without warning for her. Her housekeeper had had the day off and Matias had had no idea what sort of things his mother might need. He had opened drawers and scooped out what seemed to be appropriate clothing and in doing so had scooped out those unopened letters bound with an elastic band.

His mother's writing. He had recognised that instantly just as he had noted the date on the stamps. They had all been sent over a period of a few weeks at a time when his father had been taking what were to be his last breaths before the cancer that had attacked him two years previously had resurfaced to finish what it had begun.

Curiosity had got the better of him because

all those letters had been addressed to the same man. James Carney.

In actual fact, he need only have opened one of the letters because they had all contained the same message.

A plea for help. A request for money for an experimental treatment being carried out in America for precisely the sort of rare cancer his father had contracted. None of the letters had been opened—they had just been returned to sender. It was plain to see that the man who had defrauded Matias's family and reaped the financial rewards that should have, at the very least, been shared with his father, had not had the slightest interest in what his mother had wanted to say to him.

Carney had been too busy living it up on his ill-gotten gains to give a damn about the fate of the family who had paid the price at his hands.

There and then, Matias had realised that retribution was no longer going to be on the back burner. It was going to happen hard and fast. The time for dragging his feet was over.

If Carney's illegitimate daughter now found

herself caught in the crossfire then so be it. He wasn't going to lose his focus and the woman sitting opposite him was all part of his bigger plan. He could bring the man down the routine way, by bankrupting him, but he was getting a feeling…that there was more to the saga of his hidden daughter than met the eye. What could she tell him? Any whiff of a financial scandal, any hint that the health of his ailing company was tied up with fraud, would be the icing on the cake. Not only would such public revelations hit Carney where it hurt most, but a long prison sentence would loom on the horizon for him. All in all, a thoroughly satisfying outcome.

'Julie, my partner, wouldn't agree with you.' Sophie stuck her chin out at a mutinous angle. 'I've left her barely coping with one of the biggest contracts we've managed to secure since we started our catering company. We could really harm our business if she doesn't succeed because one poor job has a knock-on effect in the catering world.'

'You don't have my sympathy on that score,' Matias told her bluntly. He was unwillingly fascinated by the way she coloured up when she spoke and the way her aquamarine eyes, fringed by the lushest lashes possible, glittered and sparkled like precious gems.

Her skin was as smooth as satin and she didn't appear to be wearing a speck of make-up. She oozed *natural* and if he wasn't the cynical guy that he was, he would be sorely tempted to take her at face value because that face appeared so very, very open and honest.

Step up the memory of the ex who had almost got his ring on her finger on the back of appearing open and honest! Good job he wasn't the sort of idiot who ignored valuable learning curves.

'Here's a free piece of advice…never go into business with anyone. However, considering you've passed that point, you should have made sure that you weren't going into business with dead wood. Have you got anything signed allowing you to disentangle yourself from a ruinous partnership without feeling the backlash?'

Two bright patches of colour stained her cheeks and she glared at Matias without bothering to conceal a temper that was rarely in evidence. She looked at him, furiously frowning, all the more irate because he returned her glare with a lazy, amused smile. Her skin tingled as he held her gaze and kept on holding it, sucking the breath out of her and making her agonisingly aware of her body in ways that were confusing and incomprehensible.

Her breasts felt heavy and *full*, her nipples were suddenly sensitised, their tips pebble hard and scratchy against her bra, and there was a tingling between her legs that made her want to touch herself.

Sophie was so shocked that she looked away, heart hammering hard, barely able to breathe normally.

What on earth was going on with her? It was true that she hadn't had any interest in men since she had broken up with Alan, but surely that wouldn't make her susceptible to a man like Matias Rivero? He epitomised everything she disliked and if he was, physically, an attractive guy then surely she was sensible enough to be able to get past outward appearances?

'Julie is *not* dead wood,' she denied in a voice she barely recognised.

'If she's panicking because you're not there to hold her hand, then she's incompetent.'

'Thank you for your advice,' she said with sugary sarcasm, 'although I won't be paying much attention to it because I actually haven't asked for it in the first place.'

Matias burst out laughing. Against all odds, he was enjoying himself with the one person on the planet he should have wanted to have as little to do with as possible. Yes, he was on a fact-finding mission but he hadn't anticipated having fun as he tried to plumb her depths for some useful information on her father.

'Would it shock you to know that I can't think of anyone who would dare say something like that to me?'

'No,' Sophie told him with complete honesty and Matias laughed again.

'No?'

'Men with money always surround themselves with people who suck up to them and, even if they don't, people are so awed by money that they change when they're around rich people. They behave differently.'

'But you're different from them?' Matias inserted silkily. 'Or are you just someone who can afford to make penury their career choice because there has always been a comfort blanket on which to rely should push actually come to shove?'

'I don't expect you to believe me,' Sophie muttered. 'James supported us because he had to. I was grateful for that, but there was never any question about there being any comfort blanket for the…for us…'

Matias looked at her narrowly, picking up *something* although he couldn't quite be sure what.

'Because he had to…' he murmured. 'You're not exactly singing his praises with that statement.'

'But like you said,' Sophie pointed out quickly, 'he could have just walked away from his responsibility.'

'Unless…' Matias let that single word hang tantalisingly in the air between them.

'Unless?' Sophie gazed at him helplessly and thought that this was what it must feel like to be a rabbit caught in the headlights. There was something powerful and *inexorable* about him. His head was tilted to one side and his midnight-dark eyes were resting lazily on her, sending little arrows of apprehension racing through her body like tiny electrical charges.

'Unless he felt he had no choice...'

Sophie stilled. She was caught between the devil and the deep blue sea. Tell him everything and he would have nothing to do with her father, who would probably have to declare bankruptcy if everything he said was true, and where would that leave Eric? Yet say nothing and who knew where this conversation would end up?

She remained resolutely silent and thought frantically about a suitable change of subject. Something innocuous. Perhaps the weather, although that alert expression in Matias's dark, brooding eyes didn't augur well for some inconsequential chit-chat at this juncture.

He looked very much like a dog in possession of a large, juicy bone, keen to take the first bite.

'Is that it?' he pressed softly. 'Did your mother apply a little undue pressure to make sure she was taken care of? Is that the relationship you have with your father now? I expect a man like him, in a reasonably prominent position, might have found it awkward to have had the mother of his illegitimate child making a nuisance of herself.'

Lost for words, Sophie could only stare at him in absolute silence.

How on earth had he managed to arrive at this extremely accurate conclusion? And more to the point, how had the conversation meandered to this point in the first place?

'I thought you might have been the secret child he spoiled, bearing in mind his marriage failed to produce a suitable heir.' Matias was shamelessly fishing and not at all bothered at Sophie's obvious discomfort.

'I really don't want to talk about James,' Sophie eventually said, when the silence had become too much to bear. 'I know you're interested in finding out what you can before you sink money into...er...his company, but you're really asking the wrong person when it comes to business details and I don't feel comfortable discussing him behind his back.' Something her father had said, in the rush of anger, rose to the surface of her addled brain…something about *where* all the money he had given them over the years had come from, a paper trail that should have been brushed under the carpet but was threatening to re-emerge under the eagle eyes of independent auditors. She shivered.

Matias debated whether to press the issue or fall back on this occasion and he decided that, with time on his hands, there was no point trying to force her into revealing secrets that might be lurking just below the surface.

For sure, something wasn't quite right but he'd discover what that was sooner or later.

In the meanwhile…

'Is there anything you need to know about the job?' he asked briskly, finally changing the subject to her obvious relief. The details could very well be left to his head housekeeper, who was busy with preparations in the vast house somewhere, but Matias was drawn to continuing the conversation with her.

His life had become very predictable when it came to women. He had made one youthful mistake, had learnt from it and ever since his relationships had all had two things in common. One was that they followed exactly the same pattern and the second was that they were all short-lived.

The pattern involved mutual attraction with the expected lavishing of expensive presents, in something of a brief courtship ritual, followed by a few weeks of satisfying sex before he began getting bored and restless.

It didn't matter who he dated or what sort of woman happened to catch his eye. From barrister to catwalk model, his interest never seemed to stay the course.

Was Sophie right? People behaved differently in the presence of the powerful, influential and wealthy. Were the women he dated so awed by what he brought to the table that they were unable to relate to him with any kind of honesty?

Unaccustomed to introspection, Matias, for

once, found himself querying how it was that he was still so resolutely single at his age and so jaded with the revolving door of relationships he enjoyed. When had no-strings-attached fun turned into liaisons that seemed to get shorter and shorter and become less and less satisfying?

He frowned, disconcerted by this *breach of protocol* and refocused on the woman in front of him.

'Would you be able to help me if I had any questions?' Sophie quipped and he dealt her a smile that was so sudden and so devastating that she had a moment of sheer giddiness.

She blinked, owl-like, mouth parted, her cheeks tinged with delightful colour.

She wasn't angry...she wasn't defensive...she wasn't on the attack...

She was *aware*.

Matias felt that kick of his libido again, forbidden, dangerous but, oh, so pleasurable.

It had been a little while since he had had a woman. His most recent girlfriend had lasted a mere two months, at the end of which he had been mightily relieved to see the back of her because she had gone from compliant to demanding in record time.

Was his brief sexual drought generating a reaction that was as thrilling as it was unexpected?

There was certainly something undeniably sexy about Sophie and he couldn't put his finger on it. Maybe it was because he knew that he shouldn't go anywhere near her.

A thought entered his head like quicksilver. Why not? She was attractive. Indeed, it was a while since he had had his interest sparked by a woman who appeared to be uninterested in the usual game playing. There had been no coy looks, fluttering lashes or suggestive remarks. Admittedly, she was here under duress because he had placed her in an impossible situation, but even so she was doing a good job of keeping him at arm's length.

Matias watched her with brooding interest. If he wanted information on the Carney man, then surely pillow talk would yield everything he wanted to know?

Just like that, his imagination took flight and he pictured her in his super-king-sized bed, her tangle of long white-blonde hair spread across his pillow, her voluptuous pale nakedness there for his enjoyment. He wondered what her abundant breasts might look like and he imagined suckling at them.

An erection as solid as steel made him twinge in discomfort and he did his utmost to drag his mind away from imagining salacious, tawdry details about her.

'You're right,' he drawled, settling further into the chair, his big body relaxed, his hands loosely linked on his lap, his long legs extended to one side. 'If you want help, you're going to have to talk to my housekeeper. I have next to no interest in the workings of a kitchen, as I've already mentioned.'

'How lovely for you to be in a position like that,' Sophie said politely, still reeling from the way he *got to her* and made her whole body vibrate and rev up and behave almost as though it didn't belong to her at all.

'In case you're thinking that I was born with a silver spoon in my mouth, you're wrong.' He frowned because it wasn't in his nature to tell anyone anything about him that wasn't strictly essential. He didn't do confiding, especially not in women who could take one small slip-up and celebrate it as a signpost to the nearest bridal shop.

'I never said that,' but Sophie had the grace to blush because she'd certainly been thinking it. Rich, arrogant and privileged from birth had been her assumption.

'You have a very transparent face,' Matias told her wryly. 'You don't have to spell it out. It's there in your expression of disapproval. You think I'm an arrogant, ruthless tycoon who has it all and has never suffered a day's hardship in his entire life.'

Sophie didn't say anything. She was busy trying to get her body to behave and to look past Matias's devastating and unwelcome sex appeal. However, no matter how hard she tried to tell herself that she was only responding the way any normal, healthy young female would respond to a guy who would have been able to turn the head of a ninety-year-old woman with failing eyesight, she still could scarcely believe that he was capable of having that huge an impact on her.

To combat the drag of her disobedient senses, she even did the unthinkable and disinterred the mental image of her ex, Alan Pace. On paper, he had been the perfect life partner. Sandy-haired, blue-eyed and with just the sort of even, friendly disposition that had made her feel safe and comfortable. Sophie had really begun to nurture high hopes that they were destined for the long run.

She was always careful to vet the people she introduced to her brother; when, after three months, she'd filled Alan in on Eric, he had been surprised that she hadn't said anything sooner and had been happy to meet him.

Unfortunately, meeting Eric had marked the beginning of the end for them. Alan had not been prepared for the extent of her brother's disabilities and he had been quietly horrified at the thought that taking Eric out was a very regular activity and one which Sophie enjoyed and did without complaint. He had envisaged the possibility of him having to become a joint carer at some indeterminate point in the future, and although Sophie had squashed that suggestion because Eric was very, very happy where he was, she had not been able, in all good conscience, to rule it out altogether. After that, it had just been a matter of time before Alan had begun heading for the nearest exit.

Yet harking back to Alan, she had to admit to herself that not even *he* had affected her the way Matias seemed capable of doing. And before it all went belly up, Alan had been the perfect boyfriend! So what the heck was going on with her?

Not only was the man gazing at her with dark-eyed intensity very much *not* the perfect *anything*, but the last thing she felt in his presence was *safe and comfortable*.

Privately Sophie was appalled that she might bear any resemblance to her wayward mother, who had spent a lifetime making all the wrong choices and going for men just like the one sitting opposite Sophie, men who had *Danger, health hazard* stamped all over their foreheads in bright neon lettering.

'It doesn't matter what I think of you,' she said quickly, because this was the only way she could think of to bring their interaction to an end and she desperately wanted to do just that. 'I'm here to do my duty and now, if you'll excuse me, might I go and freshen up? And then perhaps I could talk to the person I will be working alongside? Also someone who can show me how everything works here?'

He was being dismissed! Matias didn't know whether to be amused or outraged.

He stood up, as sleek and graceful as a panther, and shoved his hands in the pockets of his trousers.

Sophie looked away. She knew that her face was bright red and that she was perched on the edge of her chair, rigid with tension and so aware of him that she could hardly breathe. He was just so staggeringly good-looking that she had to consciously *not* look at him and even *not* looking at him was making her go all hot and cold.

'Excellent idea,' Matias drawled, his keen eyes taking in every sign of her discomfort and also the way she was pointedly avoiding his eyes. He felt the thrill of a challenge and was already circling it, playing with thoughts of what happened next in this little scenario. 'Wait here. I will ensure that you are shown the workings of the kitchen and then to your quarters, which I trust you will find satisfactory.'

And then he smiled, slowly and lazily, and Sophie gave a jerky nod of her head, but he was already turning and striding out of the kitchen.

CHAPTER FOUR

SOPHIE HAD ONLY dimly speculated on what a long weekend party might be like. She had mostly thought along the lines of one of those upper-class country affairs where a dozen people wafted around in flowing robes, smoking cigarettes in long cigarette holders and talking in low, restrained, cut-glass accents. She had seen stuff like that in period dramas on television. Generally speaking, there was always an unfortunate death at some point.

Matias's party, she could tell as soon as guest number one had arrived, was not going to be quite like that.

Through the kitchen windows, which overlooked the spread of lawns at the back of the house and the long avenue and courtyard where the cars would be parked, the first guests arrived in a roaring vintage car, which disgorged a couple who could have stepped straight out of a celebrity magazine.

Debbie, the lovely housekeeper in her fifties who had, the day before, showed Sophie the ropes, had been standing next to her and she had said, without batting an eyelid, that everyone in the village had been waiting for this party with bated breath because the guest list was stuffed full of celebrities.

And so Sophie had discovered as the day had continued and the guests had begun piling up. All told, there would have been getting on for eighty people. Many would be staying in three sumptuous hotels in the vicinity, where chauffeurs were on standby to take them there at the end of the evening and return them to the house in time for breakfast and whatever activities had been laid on.

Through a process of clever guesswork, Sophie deduced that this wasn't so much a weekend of fun and frolic with Matias's nearest and dearest, but something of a business arrangement. The scattering of A-list celebrities from the world of media and sport was interspersed with a healthy assortment of very rich, middle-aged men who oozed wealth and power.

Sophie guessed that this was how the fabu-lously wealthy did their networking.

The supply of food was constant, as was the champagne. Having had a brief respite the day before, when Matias had done as asked and in-troduced Sophie to the people she would be working with, Sophie had been hard at it since six that morning.

Brunch was the first thing on the menu. An elaborate buffet spread, then tea before supper made an appearance at seven-thirty in the eve-ning.

Sophie had no idea what these people did when they weren't eating and she didn't have time to think about it because she was rushed off her feet cooking and giving orders and hoping and praying that nothing went wrong.

She didn't glimpse Matias, even in passing. Why would he venture into the bowels of the kitchen where the lowly staff were taking care of his needs when he had the movers and shak-ers there to occupy him? Strangely Art, Matias's employee, *had* put in an appearance in the kitchen and he had been as lovely as she recalled. Kind, gentle, almost making her think that there might be a purpose to his surprise visit, even though he had just briefly passed the time of day with her. And she wasn't quite sure why Matias had made sure to make the distinction that Art was only his *employee*, because it was clear, reading between the lines, that the two had a close bond, which, in turn, made her feel, stupidly and disturbingly, that Matias couldn't possibly be the cruel ogre she thought him to be. Didn't people's choice of friends often tell a story about *themselves*? Crazy.

Nose to the grindstone, she nevertheless still found herself keeping an eye out for Matias just in case he put in an appearance and when, at a little after eleven that evening, she made her way up to her quarters, she was foolishly disappointed not to have seen him at all.

Because she needed to make sure that everything was on target for her repaying some of the stupid debt she owed him, she reasoned sensibly. She had worked her butt off and she wanted to know that it hadn't been in vain, that day one had definitely wiped out the amount that had been agreed on paper.

The last thing she needed was to be told, when it was all over and done with and she'd shed a couple of stone through sheer stress, that he wasn't satisfied or that he'd had complaints about her or that the food had given his guests food poisoning and so she would have to cough up the money she owed him even if it meant her going bust.

She, herself, had no idea what the reaction to all her hard work was because she didn't emerge from the bowels of the wonderfully well-equipped kitchen for the entire day and night.

Waiters and waitresses came and went and an assortment of hired help made sure that dirty crockery was washed and returned for immediate use.

In addition to that plethora of staff on tap, Sophie also had a dedicated sous chef who was invaluable and did all the running around at her command.

But it was still exhausting and she had two

more days of this before the first of the guests would start departing!

Surely, she thought, she would see Matias *at some point*! Surely he wouldn't just leave her to get on with it without poking his nose into the kitchen to see whether he was getting his pound of flesh!

It was simply her anxiety given the circumstances that resulted in Matias being on her mind so much.

She was cross with herself for letting him get under her skin. She recalled the way her body had reacted to his with a shudder of impatience. He'd given her the full brunt of his personality in all its overpowering glory when there had been no one else around, but now that he was surrounded by his cronies he couldn't even be bothered to check up on her and make sure he was getting value for money.

It infuriated her that, instead of being relieved that he wasn't hovering over her shoulder or popping up unexpectedly like a bad penny, she was disappointed.

By the time the festivities were coming to an

end and the end of the long menu was in sight, she had reconciled herself to the fact that she would leave without seeing Matias at all and would probably find out the outcome of this exercise in repaying the money she owed him via his secretary.

He'd made his appearance and he wasn't going to be making another one.

She hadn't even had a chance, with everything happening, to have a look around the house! Not that she'd wanted to mingle with the guests. She knew her place, after all, but she'd hoped that she might have had a chance, last thing at night, to peep into some of the splendid rooms. No such luck because there had always been someone around or else the sound of voices from one of the rooms had alerted her to the presence of people who seemed to think nothing of staying up until the early hours of the morning.

The guests finally departed during the course of Monday in a convoy of expensive cars. The sound of laughter and chatter filtered down to the kitchen where most of the hired help had tidied, cleaned and left to go back to the village, where they would no doubt regale their family and friends with excited tales about what and who they'd seen.

Had Matias gone? By five-thirty, with just Sophie and Debbie left on the premises doing the final bits of tidying, she knew that he had. Without telling her how she had performed.

For some reason, she was booked to remain in the sprawling mansion until the following morning, and she had naturally assumed that there would be guests to cook breakfast for on that morning, but now she realised that she had been kept on to do cleaning duties after the guests had left.

He'd bought her lock, stock and barrel. She hadn't been asked to simply prepare meals, which was her speciality, but he had also kept her on to do basic skivvy work and he knew that she had no choice but to comply.

'You take the left wing of the house,' Debbie told her kindly. 'I've checked and all the guests have gone. There shouldn't be anything much to do at all because the rooms have all been cleaned on a daily basis. This is just a last-minute check to make sure nothing's been forgotten…and you've been saying that you wanted to have a peep at some of the rooms. It's worth a look. Mr Rivero doesn't come here very often but it's always a treat for us when he does because it's such a grand house.'

Finally back in her comfortable jeans and tee shirt, Sophie decided to do just that. Having not stuck her head over the parapet for the past three days, she took her time exploring the various rooms she had been allocated.

Debbie had been right: there was hardly any tidying to be done at all. Rooms had already been cleared of debris and vacuumed. She wound her way up the marble and glass staircase, admiring the canvasses on the walls as she began checking the bedrooms on the first floor.

The house looked untouched, having been completely tidied by a small army of staff.

Her mind was a complete blank as she pushed open the final door at the end of a long corridor that offered spectacular views of the lake from behind vast floor-to-ceiling panes of reinforced glass.

The first thing she noticed was the feel of pale, thick carpet under her feet as most of the house was a mixture of marble, wood and pale, endless silk rugs. Automatically, she kicked off her sandals and then stepped forwards.

Her eyes travelled to the huge bed…the white walls…the chrome and glass built-in wardrobes…the window that was just one massive pane of glass, uninterrupted by curtains or even shutters, through which Nature in all its lush green glory stretched towards the still black waters of the lake.

Then, to the left, a door she hadn't even noticed because it so cleverly blended into the pale paint opened and she was staring at Matias.

In pure shock, she took a few seconds to appreciate that he was semi naked. Obviously, he had just had a shower. His dark hair was still damp and a white towel was loosely draped around his lean hips. Apart from that scant covering…nothing. Bare chest, bare legs, bare *everything else*.

Sophie wanted to look away but she couldn't. Her mouth fell open and her eyes widened as she took in the broad muscularity of his shoulders, the width of his hard chest, the arrowing of dark hair down towards that low-slung towel. He was so absurdly, intensely *masculine* that all the breath left her in a whoosh.

She knew that she was staring and she couldn't do a thing about it. When she finally looked him in the face, it was to find him staring back at her, eyebrows raised. 'Inspection over?'

Matias had made a point of steering clear of her for the past few days. He'd regrouped and realised that what he had viewed as an interesting challenge that could lead to a number of pleasurable destinations with Sophie was in fact a poorly thought-out plan generated by a temporary lapse in his self-control.

She might be intensely attractive and he might very well be able to rationalise his visceral response to her, but taking her to his bed could only be a bad idea. Yes, pillow talk might result in him hitting the jackpot when it came to finding out more about Carney but there had been no point kidding himself that that had been the overriding reason for his sudden desire to act like a caveman and get her between the sheets.

She'd done something to him, cast some spell over him that had made him lose his formidable self-control and that wasn't going to justify whatever jackpot it might or might not lead to.

So he'd kept away. He'd even considered sleeping with one of the single women who had been at the party, a model he had known briefly several months previously, but in the end had ditched the idea.

Because having entered his head, Sophie had stubbornly lodged there like an irritating burr and he'd found he didn't want anyone else.

And now here she was. His dark eyes roved over her flushed face and then did a quick tour of her body. These were obviously the clothes she was most comfortable in and she looked sexy as hell in them. The faded jeans clung to her curves like a second skin and the tee shirt revealed breasts that were gloriously abundant.

The kick of his libido demolished every single shred of common sense. Matias had no idea what it felt like to operate without self-imposed boundaries. He was finding out now as he looked at her and surrendered to a surge of lust that could not be forced into abeyance.

The thrill of a challenge waiting to be met was one that wasn't going to go away until it was dealt with.

He padded across to the bedroom door and quietly shut it and Sophie's head swung round in alarm.

'What are you d-doing?' she stammered, frozen to the spot.

'I'm closing the door,' Matias told her gently. 'In case you hadn't noticed, I'm not exactly dressed for visitors.'

'I was going to leave…' Sophie shuffled a couple of paces back but it was laborious, like swimming against a strong current. 'I had no idea that you were still here.'

'Where else would I have been?'

'I thought you'd left with all the other guests.'

'And not had a talk to you about your performance?'

'Have I done something wrong?' Sophie asked in a rush, red as a beetroot, torn between wanting to flee and needing to stay to hear whatever criticisms of her work that he had.

Matias didn't answer. He turned around and headed towards his wardrobe and Sophie broke out in a film of nervous perspiration.

'I'd rather talk to you...s-somewhere else,' she stuttered. 'If I'd known you were in here, I would never have entered.'

'I make you uncomfortable,' Matias said flatly, spinning round to look at her and at the same time throwing on a snowy white shirt without yet removing the towel. He didn't button it up but left it hanging open over his fabulous chest and Sophie's mouth went dry.

'You're barely clothed,' she pointed out breathlessly. 'Of course I feel *uncomfortable* and I certainly don't imagine I'll be able to have a conversation about my duties in your bedroom!' She went a shade redder. 'What I *mean*...is that this is...*isn't* the place for a serious conversation. If I've failed in the task you set me, then... then...' She looked in horror as he hooked one finger over his towel.

She turned away and Matias laughed softly.

Okay, so the woman had somehow reduced him to a level of dithering unheard of. Normally, he approached women and relationships with just exactly the same assured directness with which he approached work. Both were a known quantity and neither induced anything in him other than complete certainty of the outcome.

But with *her*...his taste for revenge had been diluted by desire. What should have been clear-cut had become cloudy. He had vacillated like a hapless teenager between pursuit and withdrawal and had tried to reclaim the loss of his prized self-control only to find it now slipping out of his grasp.

He'd acted out of character and that disturbed him because it never happened.

'You haven't failed,' he said quietly. 'If you give me five minutes, I'll meet you downstairs in the kitchen and we can debrief.'

He headed towards the en-suite bathroom and Sophie fled back down the stairs to the kitchen where she had to take a few seconds to regain her self-control. She was sipping a glass of water when the kitchen door slid open and there he was, drop-dead gorgeous in a white shirt cuffed to the elbows and a pair of black jeans that showed his powerful body off to perfection.

'Have something a bit more exciting than water.' He headed straight for the oversized wine cooler and extracted a bottle of wine and then two glasses. 'You must feel as though you need it. I've thrown you in at the deep end and you've risen to the occasion.' He poured them both a glass of wine, sipped his and then, eyes on her face, tilted his head in a salute.

Sophie cleared her throat. 'Were you expecting me to fail?'

'I thought you would pull through. I didn't think that you would handle the situation with such efficiency. Everyone raved about the food and I was impressed with the way the timetable was adhered to.'

'Thank you.' She blushed and drank some of the wine.

'Naturally, the past few days only cover a proportion of the debt but you've made a start.'

'Will you be in touch about…er…another arrangement so that I can try and schedule my jobs accordingly? Julie did very well handling the cocktail party on her own but she was very nervous and I would rather not put her through that. If I know when you need me, then I can make sure I'm only missing food preparation on the premises rather than in situ at a client's house.'

'No. I can't tailor my timetable to suit your partner, I'm afraid.' He paused, gazed at her, again felt the fierce kick of desire and wondered how he could have been sufficiently short-sighted to have imagined that he could make it disappear on command. It would disappear but only after he'd had her, only when he'd sated a craving that made no sense and had sprung from nowhere. 'Did you enjoy the long weekend?'

'I was under a great deal of pressure,' Sophie confessed stiffly. 'But it was challenging catering for that amount of people. It was the largest party I've ever done.'

'I didn't see you put in an appearance.'

'I was busy overseeing the food. Besides...'

'Besides?'

'What would I have done out there? Asked everyone if they were enjoying the food?'

'You could have circulated, handed out your business cards.'

'I would have felt awkward,' Sophie admitted truthfully. 'Those sort of big bashes aren't my thing. I wouldn't have fitted in.'

'You underestimate your…charms,' Matias said softly. 'I imagine you would have fitted in a great deal better than you think.'

Sophie looked at him and wondered whether she was imagining *something* in his voice, something low and speculative that was sending a shiver down her spine and ratcheting up her painful awareness of him and her heightened reaction to his proximity. Was he actually *flirting* with her? Surely not.

Confused, she stared at him in silence and he stared right back at her, holding her gaze and making no effort to look away. He sipped his wine, gazed at her over the rim of the glass and the effect was devastating.

She was utterly defenceless. She didn't know what he was playing at. This made no sense at all. She was lower than the hired help! She was the hired help plus some!

'I sh-should head upstairs,' she stuttered, half standing on wobbly legs. 'If it's all the same to you, there's nothing left here for me to do. Er… and…if you're satisfied with…with my efforts… then maybe your secretary…can contact me…'

She ran her fingers through her tangled hair and licked her lips because *he was still looking at her with that brooding, veiled expression and it was doing crazy things to her nervous system*.

'And if…if it's okay with you, then I shall get a cab to the station tonight. I was under the impression that there would be some guests here until tomorrow morning, which is why I was… ah…booked to stay for one final night…' She took a deep breath and exhaled slowly. 'I wish you wouldn't stare at me like that,' she said, licking dry lips.

'Why?'

'Because it makes me feel uncomfortable.'

'Funny, I've never had any complaints from a woman because I haven't been able to keep my eyes off her. On the contrary, they're usually at great pains to make sure that they position themselves directly in my line of vision in the hope that I'll notice them. This is the first time I can genuinely say that I've found myself in the presence of a woman I can't seem to stop looking at.'

Shocked, Sophie literally could find nothing to say. Her vocal cords had dried up. All she could do was stare. He was so ridiculously beautiful that it seemed utterly mad for him to be saying this sort of stuff to her. Even more crazy was the fact that her whole body was surging into overdrive and melting like wax before an open flame.

She wasn't this person! She was level-headed and practical and she knew when and where to draw lines. Not that she had had to draw any since her break-up with Alan. Since then, and that had been over three years ago, men had been put firmly on the back burner and she hadn't once been tempted to dip her toes back into the dating pool. Not once. So why was her body on fire now? Because a guy with too much money, too much charm and too much in the looks department was coming on to her?

'Don't you feel the chemistry between us as well?'

'I don't know what you're talking about,' Sophie whispered and Matias raised his eyebrows in an expression of frank incredulity.

'Of course you do,' he corrected her casually. 'Although,' he continued, 'I understand that you might want to deny it. After all, it's not exactly something either of us bargained on, is it?' No truer words spoken, Matias thought wryly. All things considered, he would have placed greater odds on him catching a rocket to the red planet.

He shrugged eloquently. 'But there you are. These things happen.'

So he fancied her and wanted to have sex with her. Sophie's brain finally cranked into gear and anger began building inside her with the force of suppressed molten lava. He was a rich, powerful man who had her on the run and, because of that, he figured he could come onto her because he happened to find her attractive.

And the worst thing was that he had picked up vibes from her, vibes that had informed him that the pull was mutual. But if he thought that she was now going to fall into bed with him then he had another think coming!

'I'm sorry,' she said coldly, 'but I'm not interested.'

Matias laughed as though she'd cracked a hilarious joke. 'Telling me that you don't feel that electric charge between us?' He noted the blush that crept into her cheeks. 'Ah, yes. Of course you do. You're feeling it now. Why deny it?'

'I won't be…doing anything with you.' She wanted to walk through that door, head held high with contempt and hauteur, because he could buy her services but he *couldn't buy her*, but her feet were nailed to the ground and she found herself standing up but going nowhere. 'You're mistaking me for one of those women who *plant themselves in your line of vision*,' she continued, voice shaking with anger and mortification, 'but I'm not. Yes, I'm here because there's no other way I can pay off the money I owe you, and I can't let my colleague down because she would stand to lose out financially, just as I would if you called the debt in, but that doesn't give you the right to sit there and make a pass at me!'

Her feet finally remembered what they were there for and she stalked towards the door.

The sound of his voice saying her name brought her to an immediate stop. As noiseless as a predator stalking prey, he was right behind her when she spun round and she stumbled backwards a couple of steps, heart beating wildly behind her ribcage, her every sense alert to his commanding presence.

Her nostrils flared, an automatic reaction to the clean, woody scent of whatever aftershave he was wearing.

'Do you honestly think,' Matias asked in a voice that managed to be measured and yet icily condemnatory at the same time, 'that I might actually believe your body comes as part of the repayment schedule for the damage you did to my car?'

Sophie went bright red. Put like that, she could see what an idiot she'd been because when it came to women he certainly didn't need to use any unnecessary leverage. The guy could have whomever he wanted, whenever he wanted.

And he'd wanted her.

That treacherous thought slithered into her head, firing her up against her will.

'I suppose not,' she grudgingly conceded, 'but I feel vulnerable being here, singing for my supper.' She looked away and then raised her bright blue eyes to his. 'I'm not anything like those women who were here this weekend…'

Matias's eyebrows shot up. 'I didn't think you'd noticed who was here and who wasn't.'

'I saw them coming and going through the kitchen window and some of the guests came on kitchen inspection a few times over the weekend.'

'And?'

'And what? They were all clones of one another. Tall and skinny and glamorous. I assumed that one of them might have been your…er… girlfriend.'

'If I had a girlfriend, we wouldn't be having this conversation.'

'We don't even like one another,' Sophie breathed, 'and *that's* why we shouldn't be having this conversation!'

'Do you have a boyfriend?'

'What if I had? Would it make a difference?'

'Possibly.' He tilted his head to one side. 'Possibly not. Why do you compare yourself to other women?'

'I'm just saying that I'd imagine those women you asked to your house here were exactly the sort of women you normally dated…and so what would you see in someone like me except *easy availability*?' She was playing with fire but the sizzling danger of this treading-on-thin-ice conversation was weirdly and intensely seductive. It was the sort of conversation she had never in her life had before with any man.

'Want me to spell it out for you?' Matias husked. 'Because I will, although I'd rather do that when you're lying naked in my bed.' He vaguely recalled when he had originally played with the notion of getting her between the sheets because pillow talk might reveal secrets he could use to his advantage. Standing here now, with a fierce erection that was demanding release, the only talking he wanted to do in bed was of the dirty variety. In fact, just thinking about it was driving him completely nuts.

He didn't know what it was about this woman but she made him lose his cool.

'And that won't be happening,' Sophie informed him prissily, edging back, away from the suffocating radius of his powerful personality. 'Ever!'

'Sure about that?' Matias laughed softly, fired up on every possible cylinder. 'Because that's not a concept I recognise.'

'Too bad,' Sophie muttered, and then she turned tail and fled before she could get even more sucked into a conversation that was dangerously explosive and *dangerously, dangerously exciting.*

Not even the luxury of her accommodation, which still made her gasp after four nights, or the calming, long bath she had could clear her head.

Matias's dark, brooding, insanely sexy face swam in her head, stirring her up and making it impossible for her to fall asleep and when, finally, she did, it was a restless, broken sleep until eventually, lying in the darkened room at nearly two in the morning, she decided that counting sheep wasn't getting her anywhere.

She made her way as quietly as she could towards the kitchen. Aside from the security lights outside, the house was shrouded in darkness, which should have been spooky but was strangely reassuring.

She already knew her way round the kitchen like the back of her hand and there was no need for her to switch on any lights as she padded unhesitatingly towards the fridge to get some milk so that she could make herself a mug of hot chocolate. Time to find out whether it was true that hot chocolate encouraged sleep.

Stooping and reaching to the back of the shelf for the milk, Sophie was unaware of footsteps behind her and certainly, with only the light from the fridge, there were no helpful warning shadows cast so the sound of Matias's voice behind her came as a shock.

She straightened, slammed her head against the fridge shelf, sent various jars and bottles flying and stood up as red as a beetroot to confront a highly amused Matias staring down at her with his arms folded.

CHAPTER FIVE

BROKEN GLASS LAY around her. One of the jars had contained home-made raspberry jam. Sophie had remarked on how delicious it was when she had first had it on a slice of toast a few mornings ago and had been told that Mrs Porter, who lived in the village, made it and sold it in one of the local shops.

Sophie didn't think that Mrs Porter would have been impressed to see her hard work spilled all over the tiled kitchen floor like blobs of gelatinous blood. It joined several gherkins and streaks of expensive balsamic vinegar.

'Don't move,' Matias commanded.

'What are you doing here?' Sophie said accusingly, remaining stock-still because she was barefoot, but horribly aware of her state of undress. She hadn't dressed for company. It was a mild night and she had forsaken her towelling dressing gown and tiptoed downstairs in the little skimpy vest she wore on warm nights and the tiny pair of soft cotton pyjama shorts that left an indecent amount of thigh and leg on display.

Indecent, that was, if you happened to be in a kitchen with the man who had been haunting your dreams kneeling at your feet carefully picking up bits of glass.

He didn't look up at her. He seemed to be one hundred per cent focused on the spray of broken glass around her. Looks, however, could be deceiving for Matias was acutely aware of her standing there in a lack of clothing that was sending his blood pressure through the roof.

'I own the house,' he pointed out with infuriating, irrefutable logic as he continued with his glass retrieval while trying to divert his avid gaze from her fabulously sexy legs, pale and shapely in the shadowy darkness of the kitchen. 'I find that seems to give me the right to come and go as I please.'

'Very funny,' Sophie said tightly.

'I'm here for the same reason you are.' He sat back on his haunches to cast a satisfied look at his cleaning efforts, then he raised his eyes to hers and took his time looking at her. 'I couldn't sleep.'

'Actually, I was sleeping just fine.'

'Which is why you're here at a little after two in the morning?'

'I was thirsty.'

'Stay put. There are probably fine shards of glass on the ground still and I suppose I should clear up all this mess.' He seemed to give that a little thought. 'No. Scratch that. I'll leave the mess but I meant what I said about staying put and the shards of glass. Get a sliver of glass in your foot and you'll probably end up having to be taken to hospital.'

'Don't be ridiculous!' But she daren't move. Bleeding in his kitchen wasn't going to do. Coping with her embarrassing state of semi-nudity was definitely the better option. She would just have to stand here while he took his time removing every piece of glass from the floor. She could have kicked herself for being so stupid but bumping into him was the last thing she had expected.

Meanwhile, she could barely look down at herself because all she could see was her pale skin, her braless breasts, which were unfashionably big, and her nipples poking against the fine ribbing of her vest.

And all she could do was to make unhelpful comparisons in her head. Comparisons between herself and the women who had been at his party. Next to most of the women there, she was the equivalent of a walking, talking dumpling, and while none of them had been his girlfriend Sophie had no doubt that those were exactly the sort of women he went for. Long and thin with poker-straight hair and faces that seemed to resent the business of occasionally having to smile.

'This could take for ever,' Matias gritted, standing up and peering down at the floor. 'I don't have for ever.' He stepped forward and before she had time to even open her mouth in protest he was scooping her up as though she weighed nothing.

'Good job I was sensible enough to come down here wearing shoes,' he murmured, grinning as he looked down at her.

'Put me down!'

'Not until you're safe and sound and not until I make sure that those very pretty feet of yours are free from any slivers of glass…'

'I'd know if I'd stepped on glass,' Sophie all but sobbed, acutely aware of the way her scraps of clothing were rucking up everywhere. One of her breasts was practically popping out of her vest. She couldn't bear to look. She wasn't wearing underwear and she could feel the petal softness of her womanhood scraping against the side of the pyjama shorts.

And worst of all was what her disobedient body was doing. Turned on by the strength of his arms and the iron-hard broadness of his muscular chest, her nipples were tight and pinched, the rosebud tips straining against the vest, and she was so wet between her legs.

She could only hope that he didn't notice any of that on the way to her room.

She squeezed her eyes shut and didn't open them when she felt him push open a bedroom door.

'Ostrich.' Matias was fully aware of her body,

every succulent inch of it, soft and warm in his arms. He could just about see the rosy blush of a nipple peeping out. 'Why have you got your eyes shut?'

Sophie duly opened her eyes, glared at him and then, slowly but surely, it dawned on her that they weren't in her bedroom. He had taken her to a bedroom that was unapologetically male, from the chrome and glass of the fitted wardrobes to the walnut and steel of the bed, over which hung an abstract painting that was instantly recognisable, the bedroom she had frantically backed out of a few hours ago.

'Your bedroom.' She gulped, when her vocal cords finally decided to play ball.

'Let me check your feet.'

'Please, Matias…'

'Please, Matias…*what*?' He deposited her very gently on his bed, as though she were as fragile as a piece of porcelain, but he wasn't looking at her. Instead, he was once again kneeling in front of her and he then proceeded to take one foot in his big hand, to inspect it closely for wayward glass.

It was ludicrous!

But the feel of his hands on her…wreaked havoc with her senses and also felt just so…*sexy*.

Something that sounded very much like a whimper emerged from her throat and their eyes met.

Understanding passed between them, as loud and clear as the clanging of church bells on a still Sunday morning.

Desire. Loud and thick and electric and definitely mutual.

'We can't,' was what Sophie heard herself whimper, breaking the silence between them. She didn't even bother to pretend that she didn't know what was going on any more than he pretended not to recognise the capitulation behind that ragged, half-hearted protest.

'Why not?' Matias had thought about sleeping with her for his own purposes but now he couldn't remember what those purposes were because cold self-control had been replaced with a raging urgency to take her to bed whatever the cost.

'Because this isn't a normal situation.'

'Define normal.'

'Two people who want to have a relationship.'

'I won't deny that I don't do relationships, but sex doesn't always have to lead to a once-in-a-lifetime relationship.'

'Not for you,' Sophie whispered as her resolve seeped away the longer he looked at her with those dark, sinfully sexy eyes. 'But for me...' She turned away and swallowed painfully.

Matias joined her on the bed and gently tilted her head back to his. 'For you?'

'My mother wasn't careful when it came to men,' she told him bluntly. 'She was very attractive...she had that *something* that men seem to find irresistible...'

'You talk as though that *something* is something you don't possess.'

'I don't,' she said simply, raising her eyes to his and holding his gaze with unwavering sincerity. 'Men have never walked into lampposts when I sauntered past, they've never begged or pleaded or shown up with armfuls of roses in the hope that I might climb into bed with them.'

'And they did all those things for your mother?'

'She had that effect on them.'

'If that were the case, why didn't she and your father marry...considering he fathered a child with her?'

Sophie opened her mouth to tell him that James Carney had fathered more than one child but something held her back. What? Was it her fierce protectiveness over Eric? A need, born of habit, to save him from the curiosity of other people, even though he wouldn't have cared less?

Or was it a hangover from the way Alan had ended up reacting to her disabled brother?

Sophie told herself that she didn't care one way or another what a perfect stranger thought of her situation, least of all someone like Matias. She told herself that if he planned on doing business with her father, then the presence of her disabled brother wouldn't matter a jot, and yet she pulled back from the brink and swallowed down the brief temptation to spill her guts. She was a little startled that she had even been tempted to tell him at all.

'James always thought that he was too good for my mother.' Sophie hid the hurt behind that crisply delivered statement of fact. 'He was rich and he was posh and he didn't think that my mother was the right sort of woman for him.'

Matias's jaw clenched because this came as no surprise at all to him, and Sophie saw his instinctive reaction with a trace of alarm as she remembered how important it was for him to inject money into her father's nearly bankrupt company.

'It happens.' She shrugged and moved on quickly. 'You might fancy me, but you can't pretend that you don't feel the same way about me as he did about my mother. You're rich and powerful and it doesn't matter who my father is or isn't—the fact is that I have never grown up in the sort of circles you would have moved in.'

'You don't know what sort of circles I moved in as a child,' Matias heard himself say. He was uneasily aware that this was a deviation from his normal handling of any sort of *situation* with a woman. Since when had he turned into the sort of touchy-feely person who wanted to waste time talking when a perfectly good bed beckoned?

'I can guess. I'm not stupid.'

'You're anything but stupid. Although it *was* fairly stupid of you to be driving without insurance.'

'Please don't remind me.'

'My parents had no money,' Matias said abruptly. 'They should have but they didn't. I grew up as the kid on the wrong side of the tracks. I went to a tough comprehensive where I learned that the only way to get out in one piece was to be tougher than everyone else, so I was.'

Sophie's mouth fell open, partly because this was so unexpected but mostly because he was confiding in her and everything was telling her that this was a proud, arrogant man who never confided in anyone.

She felt a little thrill and her heart turned over because the unexpected confidence marked something more between them than *lust*. You didn't confide like that in someone you just wanted to take to bed and throw away afterwards.

Sophie didn't work that out in any way that was coherent or analytical. It was more of a *feeling* that swept through her and in the wake of that *feeling* she softened. *This was how barriers got broken down; this was how defences were surmounted.*

Except she wasn't thinking any of that right now, she was just ensnared by a desire to know more about him.

'Enough talking,' Matias said gruffly, meaning it. 'Because I'm rich and powerful now doesn't mean that I don't fancy you for all the right reasons.'

'Which are what?' Sophie whispered, and Matias dealt her a slow, slashing smile that sent every nerve in her body quivering in high excitement.

'You have a body I would walk over broken glass to touch,' he expanded, not touching her but wanting to with every pore in his body.

'Don't be silly.' She laughed shakily, driven to bring this whole crazy situation down to a prosaic, pedestrian place because she just couldn't quite believe that she was impressionable enough to be swept off her feet by a man like him. 'I'm short and I'm...well covered. The world is full of short, plump women like me. We're a dime a dozen.'

'You're doing it again, running yourself down. You shouldn't, because what you have is more than just a body I could find anywhere.' He laughed. 'You might think that your dear mama failed to pass on that special *something* but you'd be wrong because you definitely have it in bucketloads.'

Don't say that, something in Sophie wanted to yell, but over and above that was a hot yearning at the soft, lazy timbre of his voice and a melting feeling at the way he was looking at her. This was the sort of textbook situation she had always cautioned herself against and yet here she was, blossoming like a flower in the sunshine and wanting this inappropriate man more than she could have ever believed possible.

Belatedly, she realised that her clothes were still askew, her vest tugged down, her shorts scrunched up at the crotch. She shifted and just like that words melted away, replaced by the delicious frisson of burning desire.

Matias straightened. A full moon streamed

through the floor-to-ceiling panes of glass, casting a silvery glow through the room. She was so beautiful that he could barely contain himself. And *still* he wasn't sure what she would do if he touched her.

Or what *he* would do if he touched her and she turned away. A cold bath wouldn't begin to sort it out.

He didn't have long to ponder the problem because she took the decision right out of his hands. She reached up and stroked the side of his face, her huge eyes wide, her full mouth softly parted.

Matias caught her hand and drew her finger into his mouth. His gaze didn't leave hers as he sucked it, sucked it so that she knew that that was just how he was going to suck her nipple and, without even realising it, she responded by pushing her breasts out. Her nipples were tingling. Eyes half closed, she gasped when he slid his hand under the vest and cupped her breast.

He still had her finger in his mouth and was still sucking it, and still holding her gaze, his dark eyes lazy and hypnotic as he rolled his finger over the stiffened bud of her nipple. That was all he did and it was enough for her body to shriek into a response that was a hair's breadth away from orgasmic.

It was electrifying.

Sophie moaned. 'I want you.'

Matias held her hand, playing with the wet tip of her finger. 'Your wish is my command. You want me? Rest assured that you will have me, as hard and as often as you want.'

She'd expected him to drive into her without further ado. She could see the hunger in his dark eyes and it matched hers. He didn't. Instead, he arranged her on the bed, straddled her for a few seconds and then slowly pulled down her shorts.

She was so soft, so silky smooth, her skin so pale in the moonlight. He had to stare and even as he stared he did his damnedest to control his breathing, but he was so turned on that he had to make an effort to remember that breathing involved sucking air in and releasing it out.

In one swift movement, he stood up, holding her riveted attention, and stripped off.

Sophie had never seen anything so magnificent in her entire life. No artist would have been able to do justice to the sheer perfection of his body. A broad chest tapered down to a washboard-flat stomach and then lower, to an erection that was impressively huge, a thick, long shaft of steel that made her want to pass out because she was so turned on.

She'd had one serious boyfriend. Her level of experience was very definitely on the lower end of the spectrum and nothing had prepared her for the impact of being in the grip of true, shameless, wanton desire. Desire shorn of everything but a need to live for the moment and take what was on offer. Desire that was looking for nothing beyond the next sixty seconds and the sixty seconds after that.

Sophie would never have believed herself capable of actually *being here and being this person* because it contravened all her principles. But now that she *was* here, she felt wildly, wickedly decadent.

Naked, Matias spread apart her legs and then lowered himself to do something that felt so intimate that she froze for a few seconds.

'Problem?' he purred and she blushed madly.

'I've never had anyone do…that…'

'Then relax and enjoy. Trust me, you'll be begging for more.' With which, he flattened her thighs wide open, hands placed squarely on them, and he lowered his dark head between her legs. His tongue was delicate between her wet folds and then, delving deeper, he found and teased her clitoris until he could feel it throbbing. Her whimpers became cries mixed with moans. Her fingers dived into his dark hair. One minute, she was pushing him down to suck her harder, the next she was tugging him up and squirming in a futile attempt to control her reaction.

Sophie had never, ever felt anything like this before. She hadn't known that this level of pleasure even existed. She half opened her eyes and his dark head moving between her legs made her shudder and gasp. She bucked against his mouth as the rush of building pleasure began to consume her, began to take over her body, then she was coming and she could no more stop the crescendo of her orgasm than she could have stopped a runaway train with the palm of her outstretched hand.

She cried out and then panted and arched and cried out again as she spasmed against his mouth.

It seemed to last for ever.

'Matias…' this when she was finally back down on planet earth '…you shouldn't have…'

'Shouldn't have what?' He had moved up to lie alongside her and he tugged her so that their bodies were pressed so closely against one another that they could have been joined. 'Pleasured you? I wanted to. I wanted to taste you in my mouth when you came.'

'It's not just about me.'

'Kiss me and hold me. You're so beautiful. I want to feel your mouth on me…but first I need to taste your breasts. I've been fantasising about them for so long. I want to see if they taste the way I imagined they do.'

'You've been fantasising about my breasts?'

'It's hardly my fault that they're so damned gloriously big.'

'Too big.'

Matias propped himself up on one elbow to examine them. He circled one nipple with his finger, watched it pinch and stiffen. She had generous full breasts and her nipples were boldly defined circular discs. He leant down and delicately darted his tongue over one and then he suckled on it. It tasted better than his wildest imaginings. Sweet as nectar, yet with the tang of salt. It throbbed in his mouth as he drew it in and the touch of her hand at the nape of his neck and then curled into his hair was the most powerful aphrodisiac imaginable.

She was so headily responsive and yet she wasn't doing the usual gymnastics that so many of the women he bedded performed, gymnastics they always hoped would impress him enough to cement their staying power in his life.

Sophie was honest in all her responses and her little whimpers of pleasure carried a note that was almost of surprise, as if every touch was new and pretty sensational.

Good God, he thought, hanging on to restraint by a thread, a man could get addicted to this sort of thing. It was just as well that he was cool-headed enough to recognise this for what it was and to recognise himself for what *he* was. He was immune to being snared even by a woman who was driving him crazy.

He guided her mouth to his erection and knew, in the way she hesitated at first, that this was probably new to her as well, and that gave him a kick as powerful as a rocket launcher.

Sophie licked his shaft and enjoyed the way he shuddered. It made her feel more comfortable about coming into his mouth the way she had, with such wild abandon. Then she took him in her mouth and built up a rhythm of sucking that had him groaning out loud as his fingers tangled in her silver-blonde hair.

Her experience ran to the very basic when it came to sex. Her innocent fumblings with Alan, the guy she had thought she might end up marrying, were a thousand light years away from… *this*.

Her body was aching and yearning and tingling all over again. She released him and lay down again, her back arched, her hair fanning out on the pillow, her eyes closed. He was watching her. She could feel it and it thrilled her.

When she sneaked a peek, she blushed shyly and was tempted to cover her breasts with her hands but she didn't.

'I want you,' Matias groaned heavily and she sighed and smiled at the same time, not quite believing what they were doing but wanting more of it and wanting it *now*.

'Then take me,' she whispered.

The seconds it took for him to fetch a condom and put it on felt like hours because she was so hot for him.

She parted her legs and then the joy and pleasure of him entering her made her heart swell and turned her on in every corner of her body. He thrust long and deep and hard and built a rhythm that started slow, getting firmer and stronger until their bodies were moving as one.

She was so tuned into him…it felt as though they had been lovers for ever. She knew when he was going to come as surely as she knew when *she* was, and when he groaned and arched back, his big, powerful body shuddering, she, too, felt her own body ascending to a climax, coming along with him, moving to the same primitive beat.

Spent, Sophie lay in his arms. His breathing was still a shallow rasp and she could feel the perspiration binding their bodies, making them hot and slippery. It felt so good and she wriggled and nestled into him, enjoying the way his arms clasped around her.

Did she fall asleep? She must have done although when she drowsily opened her eyes she was still wrapped in his arms, his thigh between her legs, her breasts squashed against his chest.

Half asleep, she reached down to touch him and felt the immediate stir of his body as he came to life in her hands. He was no more awake than she was. He was warm and half asleep and so was she, and the merging of their bodies was as natural and instinctive as the rising and setting of the sun or the changing of the tides.

When she woke the following morning, the sun was creeping into the room, weak and grey. There was a fine drizzle of rain. Where was Matias? Not lying next to her. Sophie yawned and shifted, turning onto her side to find him working at the desk by the window.

Matias heard the sound of her stirring and immediately stiffened because this whole situation had unnerved him. The sex had been amazing but afterwards…

Hell, they had fallen asleep together, wrapped around one another like clambering vines. Sleeping was something he did on his own. Women lay in his bed for sex but retreated to another bed for sleep or, better still, cleared off. Yet he had thought nothing of falling asleep with her in his arms, and then, in the middle of the night, they had made love again, and without protection. He'd barely been awake and it had been the most mind-blowing experience of his life, almost dreamlike and yet at the same time so exquisitely *real*. Their bodies had joined together and fused and he'd come explosively.

And now…

'We didn't use contraception.' He swivelled to face her, his body already responding to her warm, flushed face and the peep of her soft, generous breasts. He wanted to have her again immediately and that unnerved him as well.

'Huh?'

'Last night. You woke me up and we made love without protection.'

Sophie shot up into a sitting position, pulling her knees towards her. 'I—I didn't think...' she stammered. She wouldn't be pregnant. She *couldn't* be pregnant. Alarm and dismay flooded her face. 'There's no way there could be an accident,' she shot back, eyes huge. 'It's the wrong time of the month for me...'

Was it? She was too fraught to do the maths.

'And I couldn't be *that* unlucky.'

Disconcerted, Matias frowned. 'Unlucky?'

Sophie leapt out of the bed, belatedly remembered that she was buck naked and dragged the duvet out to cover her. Having sex with no protection had catapulted him right back to the conniving girlfriend who had almost booked herself a trip down the aisle on the back of a fake pregnancy scare, but the horror writ large on Sophie's expressive face was telling a different story and as she scuttled away from him his instinct wasn't to pursue his accusations. His instinct was to chase her right back into his bed.

'Do you honestly think I would *want* to find myself pregnant by *you*?' Her voice was high and unsteady.

Matias stood up, as sleek and graceful as a panther, and as dangerous to her state of mind. 'Why are you bothering to try and cover yourself? I've seen you in your birthday suit and, besides, your left breast is out.'

Sophie looked down and was confronted by the sight of her pink nipple perkily defying her attempts at concealment. When she raised her eyes again it was to find Matias standing right in front of her. He had slipped on his boxers to work but aside from that he was gloriously naked and she almost fainted at the surge of desire that swept through her like a tidal wave.

'You don't mean it when you say that you'd be unlucky if you discovered you were pregnant by me,' he grated and Sophie glared at him.

'You're *so* arrogant.'

'You like it.'

'You're *so* not my type.'

'You like that too. It's boring when you're with someone who's just like you. Where's the excitement in that?'

'I don't want exciting. I've *never* wanted exciting. My mother wasted most of her life *wanting exciting*.'

'You're not your mother,' Matias returned without skipping a beat, settling his hands on her soft shoulders and gently massaging them. 'And you may not want *exciting* but that doesn't mean that your goal in life should be to settle for *deadly dull*. I'm taking it,' he continued, the low, lazy drawl of his voice sending shivers up and down her spine, 'that you're putting me in the *exciting* category.'

'This isn't funny, Matias!'

'It's anything but,' he agreed. 'Especially,' he surprised himself by adding, 'considering I had a narrow escape with a woman who claimed to be pregnant so that she could get me to put a wedding band on her finger.'

'What?' Sophie tried to recapture some of the anger she had felt but his fingers were doing things to her body and she was relaxing and un-bending and turning into a rag doll at his touch.

She was also, she discovered, heading back to the bed, a fact she only realised when she toppled back onto the mattress, with the duvet flying off her, leaving him in no doubt that, for all her protests, she was most definitely turned on by him. The tips of her nipples were stiff peaks and the rub of wetness between her legs was practically audible.

Matias didn't give her time to think. He'd never considered himself the sort of guy who could fall prey to the mindless demands of his body, but he was discovering that that was just the sort of guy she turned him into. It wasn't going to last longer than a heartbeat so why, he thought, shouldn't he just yield and enjoy the once-in-a-lifetime experience?

He shoved her over so that he could take up position lying next to her and before she could start protesting he slipped his hands between her legs and edged his finger into her, feeling her wetness with a soft moan of satisfaction.

'Stop doing that,' Sophie protested, squirming

half-heartedly to distance herself from his exploring fingers. 'I can't think when you do that. You're arrogant and you have a nerve implying that I would be the sort of girl who would engineer a pregnancy to try and get you up the aisle!'

'Did I imply that?'

'Yes, you did! What girlfriend?'

Matias lay back and stared up at the ceiling. 'I was young and cocky and on my way up. I thought I knew it all and could take on anything. Turned out I was no match for a woman who wanted to start at ground zero with me. She'd spotted my potential. I was already a massive earner by then and driving around like a strutting bull in a red Ferrari.'

'Obnoxious, in other words,' Sophie muttered darkly, but she was secretly won over by the way he could mock himself.

'Very,' Matias confirmed drily. 'She told me she was pregnant. Turned out she wasn't but that was something I only discovered by accident.'

'You told me I'm not my mother,' Sophie ventured, still on the defence and still smarting but wanting him so badly it hurt, 'and I'm not your ex-girlfriend.' She wasn't going to curl into him, which was what she wanted to do, but she wasn't turning away either. She couldn't.

'And now that we've established that...' he moved his hand away from the dampness between her legs to her breast and the teasing pink nipple begging to be licked '...why don't we skip breakfast and carry on with our magical mystery tour of one another?'

'I have to get back to London,' Sophie said raggedly, her body already quivering in acquiescence.

'No, you don't. Have you forgotten that you have a debt to settle?'

'Not like this!'

'No,' Matias agreed seriously, 'not like this, but I *would* like to commission you to cook me breakfast and I'm not hungry yet, at least not for food.'

'Matias...'

'I want you in my bed, Sophie, and then, when we've made love and I've pleasured you in every way I know how, I would like to employ you to prepare breakfast for me because there's still the matter of that pesky debt to be paid off. Will you do that?'

'I'll do that.' Sophie frowned. 'But when we leave here…'

Matias raised his eyebrows and teased the fluff between her legs until he could see her thoughts getting all tangled up in her head. 'Hmm…?'

'When we leave here,' she panted, giving in as he knew she would, 'none of this happened. Okay? I go back to being the caterer you employ so that I can pay off the money I owe you. It's back to business.'

'Sure,' he agreed smoothly, wanting her even more now that she was setting just the sort of rules and regulations that should, in theory, appeal to him, because they were exactly the ones he would set himself. 'But enough talking…'

CHAPTER SIX

FOR THE FIRST time since she had arrived, Sophie was able to appreciate Matias's sprawling mansion at leisure because she stayed to cook him breakfast the following morning and the morning after that.

'But I thought all the guests had gone,' Julie had proffered in a puzzled voice, when Sophie had phoned and told her the situation.

Sophie had muttered something and nothing about not all the guests having gone just yet, and what choice did she have considering she was indebted to the man and so had to do as he commanded or else face having their business dismantled like a house of Lego bricks in the hands of a hyperactive toddler.

She could just about extrapolate sufficient truth from what she had said to paper over her guilt at playing truant, because that was what it felt like.

She was preparing breakfast for Matias but that was just a nonsense excuse for what she was really doing. She was his lover and she was enjoying every second of it. Having curled up into herself after her experience with Alan, she was feeling liberated in a way she had never hoped to be. She was, she felt, on a journey of self-discovery and she had stopped asking herself how that was possible when Matias was so unsuitable. She just knew that he gave something to her, added some crazy dimension to her life that made her forget all the principles she had spent her life nurturing.

She was being reckless for the first time in her life and she was liking it.

You're not your mother, Matias had told her and she had actually listened and allowed herself to unbend and live a little without beating herself up about it. Okay, so Matias wasn't going to be around for ever but that didn't mean that she was going to suddenly develop a taste for inappropriate men. No, Matias was her walk on the wild side and why shouldn't she enjoy him while she had the chance?

He was rich, he was powerful, he was arrogant and he was self-assured to the point of ridiculous, but he was also, she had discovered, an extremely thoughtful lover, a good laugh, was weirdly tuned into her thoughts and just so, so unbelievably clever.

Hovering on the fringes of her enjoyment, however, was the looming certainty that he wouldn't be around for much longer, although when she thought about that a guilty little voice whispered in her head, *But won't he be...? After all, you'll still have to pay off the rest of your debt...maybe there'll be more breakfasts to be prepared...*

Breakfast this morning had been an elaborate concoction of eggs, spinach, ham and a hollandaise sauce on freshly baked bread.

The smell of the bread still lingered in the kitchen as Sophie tidied away the dishes while Matias reclined at the kitchen table like a lord and master, replete after having his appetite sated.

She turned around and he beckoned her across and patted his lap.

'Sit,' he commanded with a grin, watching as she sashayed towards him, fresh as a flower without make-up and sexy as hell in some cut-off faded jeans and a baggy tee shirt.

She wasn't wearing a bra. He liked her without one. He liked being able to reach out and touch her without having to go through the bother of unclasping boring fastenings.

They'd been larking around for two days like teenagers and Matias still couldn't get enough of her. He hadn't steered the conversation towards her father again. Hadn't even thought about it. The only thing on his mind had been her fabulous body and what it did to him.

'Nice breakfast,' he murmured as she settled obediently on his lap. He slipped his hand under the tee shirt, found the generous swell of her breast and the tight bud of her nipple, then he lifted the shirt and angled her so that she was straddling him and began suckling at her breast.

He had no idea what she possessed that could make him act like a horny teenager but she had it. In his saner moments, he remembered who she was and what his original plan had been in getting her to repay her debt by working for him. Unfortunately, those saner moments had been rarer than hen's teeth.

Watching her bustle about his kitchen, in a parody of domesticity that should have sent him running for the hills, had kick-started a nice little erection and sucking her nipple now was intensifying it to the point of painful.

He shifted under her and felt her smile as she reached down and found his hard shaft, holding it firmly but getting little traction because of his jeans.

Too little traction. He adjusted his big body and, reading him and responding instinctively, Sophie slid off his lap, discarding her tee shirt along the way, and then she eased off his trousers with a little help from him.

He was so beautiful he took her breath away. She couldn't believe that in a space of just a few days she had moved from novice to wanton, had blossomed under his touch like a plant given life-saving nutrients. He'd encouraged her to touch, to experiment, to wallow in his open adoration of her body. He'd been a masterful teacher. He'd lavished attention on every inch of her body and taught her just how to touch him and where to make him feel good.

Now, with his trousers and boxers in a heap on the ground, she took his thick shaft between her hands and played with him, absolutely enjoying the way he slid a little further down the chair and loving the guttural moan that escaped his lips. His hand cupped the crown of her head as she took him into her mouth and his fingers curled into her hair as she began to suck.

They were in their private paradise, a delicious bubble where they had been able to indulge their appetite for one another without interruption, a bubble in which thoughts and conjectures and *reality*, at least *for her*, had not been allowed to intrude.

She stood up, noting that his eyes were closed, those thick, lush lashes casting shadows on his razor-sharp cheekbones. His nostrils were flared. He knew what she was going to do and was lazily waiting to be pleasured.

Sophie couldn't get her jeans and underwear off fast enough. He did that to her, made her whole body agitate with an urgency to be satisfied. She was wet between her legs, dripping, aching to have him inside her.

She knew where he kept his condoms and quickly fetched one from the wallet in his trousers on the ground. They had made love without protection that one single time and never again. Now, she slipped a condom out of its foil and took him between her hands so that she could put it on him.

His eyes were slumberous on her, hotly working her up to a peak of excitement, and she groaned out loud as she lowered herself onto him, her every nerve ending tingling as he circled her waist with his big hands, then she was moving on him, pressing down to feel him deep inside her, letting him take her to places only he could.

He levered her head towards him and kissed her as she moved on him, a deep, hungry, urgent kiss that made her moan and then she was coming, hurtling towards that peak of satisfaction, her body moving in perfect rhythm with his until the world exploded and all she could feel was the intense pleasure of her climax that went on and on, subsiding eventually in little, erotic waves that left her shaking and trembling.

She sagged against him, head against his chest, listening to his slow, ragged breathing that very gradually returned to normal. They were both practically slipping off the chair and she reluctantly climbed off him and began sticking back on her clothes.

He looked so peaceful there, his big body relaxed, his eyes half closed as he watched her scramble to put on her tee shirt and then hop into her underwear.

He wasn't at all self-conscious about his body. Where, even now that they had made love what felt like a thousand times, she still needed to put on her clothes rather than parade her nudity, he couldn't care less.

He stood up, flexed his muscles and looked at her sideways with a satisfied smile.

'Work is beginning to call,' he drawled, eyeing the puddle of clothes on the ground and deigning to put on his jeans but nothing else. 'She's an extremely demanding mistress.'

'Yes, I have to get back as well.' Sophie's heart sank but she smiled brightly at him. 'Julie's beginning to tear her hair out because we've just landed a pretty big order and it's hard planning a menu together over text or on the phone.'

'You still owe me for my car...' He swerved round her and, standing behind, wrapped his arms around her waist and leant down so that he was talking into her hair, his voice a little muffled.

Sophie literally thrilled. She couldn't help grinning from ear to ear. She knew that this situation wasn't going to last and was probably the least sensible thing she could be doing but the pull of having fun was irresistible. She couldn't think beyond it.

'But,' Matias continued gravely, 'you're paying off the debt quickly. That said... I might still need you to do some catering for me and I rather enjoy the private catering you've been providing, by which I mean those excellent breakfast options you've presented to me.'

Sophie swivelled round so that they were facing one another and she looked up at him. 'I like cooking you breakfast,' she told him. 'Do we...er...put a date in the diary? How does this work?' She sighed and reached up to link her fingers behind his neck. 'I mean, Matias, how does this *really* work? Is there a time frame? And if I choose to stop...*this*...then what happens? I feel vulnerable thinking that we've entered new territory.'

'Do you think I'm going to penalise you if you decide you want to stop being my lover? I won't. I'm not that kind of guy. You're free to make your choice. I still want you, Sophie, but there's no way I want you to feel that you're somehow committed to pleasing me for fear of what I might do if you change your mind.'

The bubble was beginning to burst. They weren't going to be in one another's company twenty-four-seven, making love, talking, making love again. True, Matias had taken himself off for brief periods to work, during which time she had video called Julie so that she, too, could remember that real life was going on outside his glasshouse mansion, but most of their time had been spent in one another's company.

Living in the moment had been easy. She had been able to turn a blind eye to real life because real life was located somewhere outside the glass and concrete of his house. Real life was back in London. Well, they were returning to London soon and although she had told him that, once they left, what they had would come to an end, she didn't want it to end and that frightened her.

They hadn't mentioned actual numbers at all in terms of the money she still owed him for the damage to his car. She didn't care about that because she had discovered that, despite the fact that he could be stunningly arrogant, he was also incredibly fair and incredibly honourable.

What did concern her was the deal he was considering making with her father. That, too, was a subject that hadn't been raised, but it would be just as soon as they drove away from their little bubble and the real world started to intrude. She had promoted James Carney as someone he *should* deal with, had sidestepped most of the truth about her father because what was at stake was the fate of her beloved brother.

Suddenly it was vitally important that she tell him about Eric. She didn't have to compromise any deal Matias wanted to do with her father, but at least when the deal was done and should her father show his true colours, *which wasn't inevitable because he would be on the back foot*, Matias would put two and two together and understand why she had done what she had, why she hadn't warned him off.

Not that, Sophie feverishly told herself, there would be any problems. Her father was broke. He needed Matias. He would be on best behaviour.

'Good,' she said vaguely, wondering how to send the conversation in the direction in which she wanted it to go and finally deciding to just say what she had to say. 'And about my father...'

'Yes?' Matias's ears pricked up. He marvelled that this was the first time Carney had been mentioned in their couple of days alone together when the original purpose of her being here was to provide information that he could use. It irked him that he had been so sidetracked by her that he had taken his eye off the ball.

'Will you still…er…be interested in investing money in his company?' Sophie had the whole back story about Eric prepared for Matias and was a little taken aback at the sudden deathly silence that greeted her question.

'Ah. We haven't discussed that, have we?'

'I guess there have been a few distractions.' She laughed nervously.

'So there have.' Matias looked at her coolly, his quick brain putting two and two together and not liking what he was coming up with.

'What's wrong?'

'What makes you think that something's wrong, Sophie?'

'I don't know. What have I said? I just thought that…we're going to be leaving here and I wanted to talk about what happens next.'

'Why would that lead to a discussion of my plans for your father? But now that we're on the subject…you've, apparently, no idea about the ugly business of making money, but did you know your father is…shall we say…battling one or two financial problems…?' Matias was watching her intently and he was as still as a statue.

She knew. It was there, written plainly on her face. She'd played the clueless card, but she'd known all along that her old man was broke. She wasn't even trying to deny it.

'And,' Matias continued, testing the ground as the steady burn of rage began to build inside him, 'of course, if any deal is to go through, then there will have to be certain background checks…'

'Background checks?' she squeaked.

Matias shrugged but he was picking up everything he wanted to know and more from her reaction. 'The business community is a small world. There have been certain rumours of shady dealings…'

Sophie's face drained of colour. Her legs felt shaky. Her brain was in meltdown as she thought of what would be revealed in *background checks*. She knew nothing for sure, but she suspected…

'Surely that wouldn't be necessary,' she whispered.

'Oh, dear.' Used. He'd been used. She'd slept

with him to facilitate a deal with her father whom she knew to be penniless and crooked. She was clearly running scared from background checks that she must know could open up a can of worms. He'd got the information he'd wanted after all, but the fury of finding himself played once again was volcanic in its intensity. 'You seem apprehensive. Did you think that you could *distract* me into putting money into your bank account without doing my homework thoroughly?'

Sophie's face drained of colour as she tried to make sense of what he was saying but the dots weren't joining up. What was he implying?

Some part of her was desperate to give him the benefit of the doubt and to find a reasonable explanation for the cold, veiled expression on his handsome face but a chill was growing inside her and it make her feel sick and giddy.

'I d-don't know what you're talking about,' she stammered.

'Don't you?' Not even his duplicitous ex-girl-friend from long ago had managed to produce a rage like this. He'd learned *nothing* because he'd been conned again. If he'd smashed his fist against the wall, he would have driven it right through the brickwork, so powerful was the torrent of emotion coursing through his body. 'I don't know why I didn't stop to question your sudden departure from shy and blushing to hot and ready for sex.'

'That's an awful thing to say!'

'If memory serves me right, you had your claws out when we first met...'

'Because you were horrible to me! Because you threatened to shut down my business to pay off a debt!'

'But then we came to a satisfactory conclusion, didn't we? But when did you decide to hop in the sack with me? Was it when you found out that I might decide to have business dealings with your father? Did you think that you were clever in trying to withhold the true state of your father's coffers and the fact that he's a crook? Did you think that your sexy body would seal the deal for me regardless of that?'

Sophie stared at him round-eyed. She was looking at a stranger. Gone was the teasing, seductive guy who could turn her off and on like a light switch.

'No! I would never do something like that! The only reason I mentioned my father and…well… is because I wanted to tell you something that…'

Matias held up one imperious hand. 'Not interested. The fact is there's something you should know.' He killed the tight knot in the pit of his stomach. Sex was sex but business was business and this was the business of retribution and he'd been a fool to have ever been distracted by her gorgeous body and beautiful, duplicitous face.

Sophie was spellbound, filled with creeping dread and apprehension. He was pacing the kitchen, restless and somehow vaguely menacing in the soft prowl of his movements.

'Regrettably, you've got hold of the wrong end of the stick. The fact is, the only interest I have in your father won't be leading to any lucrative deals that might result in more money lining your pockets.' He looked at her flushed face narrowly and it got on his nerves that he half wanted her to deny that she had any interest in any of her father's money that might come her way, but she remained silent and he could tell from the expression on her face that money trickling down into her grasping little hands had been exactly what she had hoped for.

She'd turned into his compliant lover because sex was a most persuasive tool. His mouth tightened and cold hostility settled like glacial ice in his veins.

'You don't understand,' Sophie protested weakly, but everything seemed to be moving at bewildering speed and her brain couldn't keep up.

'I think I understand very well indeed. But here's what *you* don't understand. Not only will I *not* be putting money into your father's business, but my intention couldn't be more different. I won't be the making of your bankrupt, disreputable scumbag of a father. I will be the ruination of him.' He clenched his jaw as her mouth fell open and the colour drained away from her face. 'You may not remember but I mentioned in passing to you that my parents should have had money and all the little luxuries that go with the sort of well-oiled lifestyle your daddy dearest enjoyed, but sadly they didn't.'

'I remember… I meant to ask you about that… but…'

'Distractions…ah, yes, they got in the way.' Matias smiled coldly. 'Let me fill in the gaps. Your father stole my father's invention and used it to prop up the sad sack company he had inherited that was already on its last legs, and in the process made himself rich beyond most people's wildest dreams. My father was naïve and trusting, a simple emigrant who believed the rubbish your father told him about them going in as partners, jointly reaping the financial rewards of something my father invented. I know, because I've seen the proof of those conversations with my own eyes in letters that were kept in a folder. It never occurred to my parents that they could have taken the man through the courts and got what they deserved.'

'No.' But she already believed every word that was being said because that was very much the sort of thing her father would have done.

'My father never recovered from the betrayal

of his trust. What your father did infected every area of my family's life. My father died prematurely from a rare cancer and do you want to hear the worst of it? I recently found more letters, hidden away amongst my mother's things, begging letters from my mother to your father, pleading for some money to send my father to America where groundbreaking work was being done in that area, clinical trials that were beyond my parents' meagre means.'

'I'm so sorry,' Sophie whispered brokenly.

'So,' Matias rammed home, every syllable filled with icy condemnation made all the more biting because he knew that he had allowed himself to drift into territory he should never have occupied, 'my intention was always to make your father pay for what he did.'

'What are you saying?'

'I think you know. I knew about Carney's penury. I wanted more information and I got it. A stint in jail seems appropriate considering what he did, wouldn't you agree? So thank you for corroborating what I suspected. Now I know exactly which rocks to turn over when I have your daddy's company in my hands.'

A wave of sickness swept through her. She had accepted that they were ships passing in the night and had justified her extraordinary response to him on all sorts of grounds about lust and desire, but now that the extent of his deception was unravelling in front of her she knew that she had felt a great deal more for him than lust or desire.

He had managed in drawing out a side of her that she hadn't known existed. He had made her laugh and forget all the worries that plagued her. When she had been with him, she had stopped being the girl who had been let down by an ex, the girl who had to grovel for handouts, the girl with the disabled brother whom she fiercely protected, the girl whose career could crash and burn at any moment, leaving her nowhere. When she'd been with Matias, unlikely as it was, she had been carefree and sexy and *young*.

But that had been an illusion because he had used her to get information about her father out of her, and the depth of her hurt was suffocating.

'I played right into your hands with that accident, didn't I?' Her voice was stilted but despair, as toxic as acid, was filling every corner of her. 'You don't care a jot that *I* never hurt your family.' She wasn't going to try and explain anything about Eric to him now, nothing at all, and she hated herself for allowing him to get so close, close enough for her to have been tempted to open up about her beloved brother. This ruthless, unfeeling man in front of her wouldn't even care. 'Did you even fancy me?' Tears stung the backs of her eyes. She was asking questions and she didn't want to know the answers but she couldn't help herself.

Matias flushed darkly. It pained him to see the wounded hurt in her eyes but he wasn't going to be sidetracked by that. This time he was going to stick to the brief. No way was he going to let her swing the tables round and cast him in the role of the criminal. She'd been after money and that was the long and short of it, end of story.

'I should have stopped to ask myself why a man like you would have looked twice at me,' Sophie continued bitterly.

'Can you deny,' Matias intoned coldly, 'that you wanted me to pour money into your father's company because you knew that, if I did, some of it would inevitably come your way?'

Sophie closed her eyes.

She had needed that money but she would die before she explained it to him now. Instead she had to accept that she had been a tool to be exploited by him in his search for revenge. They hadn't been getting closer. That had all been in her stupid mind because he hated her for a crime she hadn't committed.

Matias noted that she couldn't even meet his eyes and he bunched his fists, resisting the urge to punch something very, very hard. He was uncomfortable in his own skin and that enraged him. He moved to the door, remained there for a few seconds, his body deathly still and yet seeming to exude a savage, restless energy.

'Our return to London will mark the end of any relationship between us.'

'But what about the money I still owe you?' Panicked, she licked her lips nervously.

'Do you honestly think that I would want to set eyes on you ever again, Sophie?'

Tears gathered at the backs of her eyes and she swallowed painfully, not wanting to cry in front of him but fearing that she would. Her heart was thundering inside her and her head was beginning to hurt.

'You're going to take my company away from me,' she said flatly. 'You don't care who you hurt in your desire for revenge. It doesn't matter that I had nothing to do with whatever my father did to your father.'

Matias's jaw clenched. His eyes drifted down from her defiant heart-shaped face to the body he had so recently taken and he was furious that, in defiance of the hostile atmosphere simmering between them, his body was still insisting on responding to hers with unbridled gusto.

He harshly reminded himself that whatever she trotted out, nothing could excuse the fact that she had tried to encourage him to open dealings with her father because she'd wanted his money. Whatever guise it took, the apple never fell far from the tree. Greed was in her blood and nothing else mattered.

'Consider the debt to me paid in full,' he gritted. 'I won't be going after your company so you can breathe a sigh of relief. I walk through this door and all dealings between us, as I've said, come to an end. I will instruct my secretary to email you confirming that you no longer owe me anything for the damage to my car and you should consider yourself fortunate, because there are no limits for me when it comes to getting justice for what your father did to mine. In life, there is always collateral damage.'

Being referred to as *collateral damage* just about said it all, Sophie thought, devastated. Thank goodness, she hadn't confided in him about Eric. Thank goodness she hadn't allowed him even further into her heart.

'I shall go and pack my stuff up and then I think I'll get a taxi to the station and take the first train back to London.'

'My driver will deliver you to your house. In the meantime, I have ignored work demands because of certain *distractions*.' His mouth curled into a sardonic smile. 'It's time for me to return to normality and not a moment too soon.'

Every word that passed his beautiful mouth was a dagger deep into the core of her but, no, she wasn't going to break down in front of him. She wasn't going to let him see how far he had already burrowed into her.

She nodded curtly and remained where she was as he turned his back on her and walked out of the kitchen.

Then and only then did her whole body sag, like a puppet whose strings had been abruptly cut.

But only for a few minutes, a few minutes during which she breathed deeply and did her best to find the silver lining in the cloud. It was what she had spent a lifetime doing. She'd done it every time she visited her brother and reminded herself that life with him in it, however damaged he was, was so much better than life without him in it. She'd done it every time she'd gone to her father, cap in hand, to beg for the money needed to keep Eric safe and happy, and left with the cash.

She would do it again now, and she would thank her lucky stars that she hadn't had the opportunity to emotionally invest even further in a guy who'd used her. And she'd thank her lucky stars that her debt to him was repaid in full.

But, as she got ready to leave, flinging her possessions in the case she had brought with her, her heart was still telling her that life was never going to be the same again.

CHAPTER SEVEN

SOPHIE LOOKED AT the innocuous white stick with the two bright blue lines and felt a wave of nausea surge through her all over again.

This was the third pregnancy test she had done and still her mind refused to compute the enormity of what was staring her in the face. She was sorely tempted to use the last one in the box but she knew that she had to accept the horrible, terrifying truth that she was pregnant. One reckless mistake had resulted in the baby growing inside her. She could do a hundred more tests and nothing was going to change that inalterable fact.

She was having Matias's baby.

A guy who had played her, used her and then discarded her without a backward glance. It had been a little over five weeks since she had last seen him, disappearing through the kitchen door of his over-the-top hillside mansion. Since then she had received a formal email from his secretary informing her that all monies owing to him had been cancelled. Since then, her father's company had gone into liquidation and was now in the process of being eaten up by Matias's sprawling empire. Sophie knew that because it had been on the news. Her father, needless to say, wanted no more to do with her because of the situation he was in. He had no more money to give her and the last time she had seen him, he had angrily accused her of helping to send him to the poorhouse. He'd conveniently overlooked the fact that the failure of his company had been down to his own incompetence and she had not reminded him, choosing instead to walk away and deal with the problems the bankruptcy presented to her brother's future.

Had Matias put the final nail in the coffin and sent the police after her father as well? She didn't know. If so, that was a further public humiliation to come.

Released from having to maintain appearances for the sake of his peers, she and Eric had been cut loose and Sophie had spent every night for the past fortnight trying to find a solution to the problem of how to keep her brother in the safe home he had grown accustomed to.

She was stressed beyond belief and now this had happened.

'You'll have to tell him,' was the first thing Julie said to her later that morning when she showed up at the house.

Sophie looked at her friend, utterly defeated and without a silver lining in sight. 'How can I?' she asked, remembering how they had parted company and feeling the stamp of pride settle in her like a stone. 'You know what happened, you know…' her voice cracked and she took a deep breath and continued in a rush '…what his motives were for getting involved with me.'

'But this is no longer about your father, Soph, or whatever revenge Matias Rivero was after. This is about a new life growing inside you that can't be made to take the blame for a situation he or she had nothing to do with.'

Sophie knew that in her heart of hearts. How could she withhold the baby's existence from his own flesh and blood? Matias would have to know but only because she could see no other way around it. She would have to make sure he knew that she *wanted nothing from him*. She didn't care how much money he had. As far as she was concerned, she would do the right thing and tell him about the baby, but after that she would walk away.

And he would be able to breathe a sigh of relief because she knew that the last person he would want to see show up at his office, again, would be her.

First time, she had shown up having crashed into his car. Now, she would be showing up with a baby-shaped wrecking ball solidly aimed at his life.

She could remember just how she had felt that first time she had shown up at his impressively scary office headquarters and spoken to the receptionist. Sick with nerves at an uncertain outcome, and yet with just enough hope that everything would be okay because although she wasn't going to be seeing the very empathetic Art Delgado, deep down she had clung to the belief that the guy she *would* be seeing might be cut from the same cloth.

One day later, as Sophie yet again stood outside the impressive building that housed Matias's legendary empire headquarters, hope was nowhere in existence.

She had had several hours to get her head round her situation and yet she was no nearer to locating any silver linings.

She strode into the glass building with a great deal more confidence than she was feeling and asked for Matias with the sort of assurance that implied an audience would be granted without argument.

'It's a personal matter,' she added to a frowning young blonde girl, just in case. 'I think Matias... *Mr Rivero*...would be quite upset if you don't inform him that I'm here. Sophie Watts. He'll know who I am and it's urgent.'

Would he see her? Why should he? His parting shot had been that he never wanted to set eyes on her again, even if that involved kissing sweet goodbye to the thousands of pounds she still owed him.

* * *

About to go to the boardroom to close a multi-million-pound deal, Matias was interrupted by his secretary and told that Sophie was in the foyer several stories below.

For approximately two seconds, he debated delivering a message back that he was unavailable.

He didn't. He'd walked away from her weeks ago but hadn't managed to escape whatever malign influence she had over him. She'd lodged under his skin like a burr, appearing like a guilty conscience just when he least needed it and haunting his dreams with infuriating regularity.

Everything was going nicely when it came to dismantling her father's company, ensuring that the man was left standing out in the cold with no shelter in sight. Behind the scenes, further revelations would come when he moved to phase two, which would involve the long arm of the law. An eye for an eye.

It should have given him an additional sense of satisfaction that his daughter, whose greed had matched her father's, would also be standing in the same cold spot, without any shelter on the horizon. Unfortunately, every time he tried to muster the appropriate levels of satisfaction at a job well done, the image of her soft heart-shaped face popped into his head, giving him pause for thought.

Revenge had been served cold, but it was not as sweet as it should have been.

It didn't help that his mother had read all about the takeover in the newspapers and had summoned him to the hospital where she was recovering nicely. She'd never agreed with his thirst for retribution and nothing had changed on that front.

All in all, he was pleased that he had done what he had done, because as far as he was concerned those wheels of justice had to turn full circle, but he was surprised at how dissatisfied he remained at what should have been a stunning victory of the present over the past. And he knew it was all down to Sophie.

'Show her up,' he told his secretary in a clipped voice, instantly deciding to put his meeting on

hold, regardless of the value of the deal. 'And tell
Jefferies and his team that Bill Hodgson will be
handling the initial closing stages.' He ignored
the startled look on her face because such an
about-face was unheard of.

His mind was already zooming ahead to what
Sophie might want from him.

Money was the first and only thing that came
to mind. She had encouraged a deal with her father so that she could benefit from the financial
injection. No deal meant no financial injection,
which meant that she still wanted money, except
it wasn't going to come from her dear papa.

He was outraged that she would try her luck
with him. He knew that he certainly shouldn't be
allowing her any chink through which she might
try and slip. But he couldn't resist the opportunity to see her and he was, he acknowledged,
curious to see what approach she would take to
try and wheedle cash out of him.

Would she shoot him one of those sweet, innocent, butter-wouldn't-melt-in-her-mouth smiles?
The kind of smile that instantly went to his groin
and induced all manner of erotic, dirty, sexy sce-

narios in his head? He got a kick imagining her sashaying into his office, hot for sex. He'd send her on her way, but he still experienced a massive surge of desire playing with the thought.

The single knock on his door found him relaxing in his chair, his hands loosely linked on his washboard-flat stomach, his expression one of mild curiosity.

'Yes.' The door opened, his secretary stood to one side and there she was, tentatively walking into his office, blushing in the way that would send any normal, red-blooded man's pulse through the roof. She was wearing a pair of grey trousers and a white blouse and his eyes immediately dropped to the soft swell of her breasts and, right on cue, his brain lurched off at a predictable tangent, remembering exactly what those luscious breasts had felt like, had tasted like. 'What have you come for?' he asked abruptly, putting paid to the raunchy turn of his thoughts. He pushed himself away from the desk but did nothing to make her feel comfortable. Why should he?

'Can I sit down?'

Matias nodded to the chair. 'I wouldn't make myself too comfortable if I were you,' he drawled. 'Time is money, after all. On the subject of which, I'm taking a stab in the dark here at the reason for your sudden, unexpected visit. Because this isn't a social call, is it?'

'No.' Her voice was steady and Sophie was proud of that, although that, in fairness, was the only part of her that felt remotely controlled. She hadn't laid eyes on him for weeks but she hadn't stopped thinking about him, and, seeing him in the flesh now, she was shocked that she could have so massively underestimated the impact of his physical presence.

His lean, dark face was even more stunningly beautiful than she recalled, his mouth more cruel, more sensuous, his body…

Sophie didn't want to think about his body. She just wanted to say what she had come to say and leave before her steady voice went the way of the rest of her. She reminded herself of the man he had turned out to be, vengeful and ruthless, and a lump of ice settled inside her, the cold knot of hatred, which she welcomed.

'Didn't think so.' Matias's lips thinned. He was recalling in vivid detail the mind-blowing sex they had shared… He was also recalling the reason she had slept with him. 'I expect you read all about your father's downfall in the financial pages.'

'You must be pretty pleased with yourself.'

Matias flushed darkly, nettled by the cool disdain in her voice. 'Your father got what he deserved.' He shrugged. 'And yes, I'm quietly pleased with myself, although I have to say that had he not let his company run aground, my job would have been considerably less easy. He was a thief, a conman and eventually an idiot who let go of the reins and never thought that the horse might bolt. A great deal of highly suspect financial dealings is being uncovered, but that won't come as any surprise to you. In due course, your father and Her Majesty will be more than nodding acquaintances, but not in the way he would doubtless like. But you haven't come here for a chat. I'm a busy man so why don't we just cut to the chase, Sophie? No deal with your father means no rescue of his terminally ill company, which means no cash in hand for you. So I'm guessing that you're here to see whether there isn't another way to elicit money out of me.'

'I wouldn't accept a penny from you if my life depended on it,' she snapped. Every word that had passed his beautiful lips stung, every word was a reminder of exactly what he thought of her.

If she could have turned tail and run for the hills, she would have, but Julie had been right. A father deserved to know about the existence of his child, even if he chose to do nothing with the knowledge. However much she hated him for how he had treated her, she was fair enough to recognise that simple fact.

'We're going round the houses here, *querida*. In one sentence, why don't you just tell me what the hell you're doing in my office?'

'We had unprotected sex, Matias. Do you remember?'

Two sentences that dropped into the still silence between them with the power of an unexploded bomb.

Usually quick on the uptake, Matias could literally feel his brain slowing down, skidding to a halt in the face of what she had said and what she hadn't.

'I remember...' he said slowly. It was strange but that languorous bout of lovemaking, in that quiet surreal lull between sleeping and waking, had stayed right there, between the sheets, trapped in a moment in time. Had he subconsciously shoved it to the back of his mind rather than face the possibility that taking her without protection might have had consequences? Or had it just seemed unreal in the light of day and therefore easily forgotten?

He was remembering now, remembering the way their bodies had fused, warm and lazy and barely awake.

'I'm pregnant, Matias,' Sophie told him flatly.

She'd not envisaged what sort of reaction she would get from her announcement. In her head, she said what she had to and then walked away. Now, as she watched the vibrant bronze of his face slowly pale, she found herself riveted to the chair into which she had sunk.

'You can't be,' he denied hoarsely.

'I've done three tests. I didn't even think about it until I started feeling nauseous every morning and realised that my period hadn't come.'

'It's impossible.' Matias raked his fingers through his hair and realised that his hand was shaking. Pregnant. She was having his baby. Just like that, his eyes darted to her still-flat stomach, then to her breasts, which now, suddenly, seemed bigger and lusher than he remembered. 'And if this is your attempt to try and get money out of me, then you're barking up the wrong tree. You seem to forget that I've had ample experience of a woman who will use a so-called pregnancy to worm her way into my bank balance.'

Sophie rose on shaking legs. 'I'm going now, Matias. I know you had a poor experience in the past and I'm very sorry that I've had to come here and spring this on you, but I'm not your ex-girlfriend, I'm not lying and I certainly don't want a penny from you. After what you did to me, do you honestly think that I could ever want anything from you? *Ever?* I'm here because I felt you should know about your baby.'

Matias watched as she began walking towards

his office door. Everything seemed to be happening in slow motion or maybe it was just that his brain had now totally seized up, unable to deal with a situation for which he had not, in any way, shape or form, prepared himself. He didn't move as she opened the office door but then he did, suddenly galvanised into action.

He caught her as she was barrelling along the corridor towards the bank of lifts and he placed his hand on her arm, forcing her to a stop.

Who cared whether his bizarre behaviour was being observed?

'Where do you think you're going?' he gritted.

Sophie's eyes flashed. 'Back home! Where do you think? I can't believe you would have the nerve to accuse me of faking a pregnancy to try and extort money out of you. What sort of person do you think I am? No. Don't bother answering that! I know already!' She yanked her arm out of his grasp and hit the button on one of the lifts, which obligingly opened at her command. She stepped in, eyes firmly averted from Matias, but she was all too aware of him stepping into the lift with her and slamming his fist on one of the buttons, which instantly brought it to a shuddering stop between floors.

'What are you doing?' Alarmed, Sophie finally looked him squarely in the eyes and then blinked and made a huge effort to drag her eyes away because, even when she was seething with hatred, she still couldn't help finding him so impossibly attractive. It wasn't fair!

'We need to talk about this and if this is the only way to get you to talk to me, then I'll take it.'

'You can't just *do that*.' Sophie was shocked because wasn't that breaking the law? Normal people didn't just *stop a lift to have a conversation*! But then since when was Matias Rivero a *normal human being*?

'Why not?'

'Because…because…'

'Are you going to have a conversation with me about this or are you going to put on your running shoes the second we're out of this lift? Because you can't drop a bombshell like that in my lap and then try and dodge the bullet.'

'I don't want anything from you,' Sophie repeated fiercely. 'I hate you!'

'Message received loud and clear.'

'And I didn't engineer getting pregnant to try and get money out of you! That's a vile thing to say even from you, but why should I be surprised?'

'Let's not waste time going down that road. It's not going to solve anything.'

'And I have no intention of getting rid of this baby, if that's what you're thinking!'

'Did I insinuate that that was what I wanted?' Matias raked frustrated fingers through his hair. Her colour was high, her eyes were glittering like aquamarines, and she was the very essence of bristling feminine fury. He set the lift back on its way down. 'We're going to go to a small wine bar five minutes' walk from this office. I know the guy who owns it. I'll make sure we get a good seat at the back somewhere and we can have a civilised conversation about this problem. Agreed?'

Sophie scowled. 'You used me just to get dirt on my father.' She looked at him narrowly and with hostility. 'We can talk about this if you like but I don't want you to forget how much I detest you for doing what you did.'

Matias hung onto his temper. He had no doubt that she was telling the truth and, with the dust settling, the grim reality of what had happened was beginning to take shape. He was going to be a father. When it came to his bucket list, having a kid had never been on it and yet here he was, with only a few months left of sweet indepen-dent singledom because of one crazy mistake.

Life as he knew it was about to undergo a seis-mic change and getting wrapped up in blame and counter-blame wasn't going to alter that.

The wine bar was half empty and they were, indeed, afforded utter privacy at the very back, where they were tucked away from the other ta-bles. Matias ordered a coffee for them both and then looked at her directly.

'When did you find out?' he asked quietly, shunning anything that might lead to another emotive outburst.

'Yesterday.' Sophie glared bitterly at him and fiddled with the handle of her cup before taking a sip and grimacing because her taste buds were no longer quite the same. 'And don't think that it wasn't as big a shock for me as well! Don't think that I haven't thought about how Fate could have been so cruel!'

'Whatever has happened in the past, we have to put behind us or else we'll be stuck on a tread-mill of never moving forward and the only way we can deal with this problem is to move for-ward towards a mutually agreeable solution.'

Sophie stared coldly at him because every word he said, while making perfect sense, left her feeling angry and defensive. Problem? Mutu-ally agreeable solution? She rested her hand pro-tectively on her stomach, a gesture that Matias keenly noted, just as he understood that tread-ing on eggshells about summed up where he was right at this moment. She had come to his office under duress and was not inclined to give him the benefit of any doubts, but she was hardly the saint she made herself out to be, he thought. She talked a lot about him using her but hadn't she been after his money? No, she wouldn't be in line for a halo any time soon, but, like it or not, he had to listen to his own words of advice and approach the situation dispassionately.

'That's easier said than done,' Sophie said tonelessly and Matias heaved an impatient sigh.

'You wanted me to engineer a deal with your father because you thought he might be able to help you financially if he wasn't in financial trouble himself. Am I right?' His voice was level and cool. 'So when you rant and rave about what a bastard I am, take a long look at yourself and try and put things into perspective.'

He hadn't wanted to raise this thorny issue be-cause he didn't see what the point of raising it might be, considering it wouldn't advance any sort of solution to their problem, but raise it he had and he was disconcerted by the absolute lack of suitable apology on her face. Clearly a sense of guilt didn't feature in her repertoire.

And yet that seemed strangely at odds with the person she came across as being. Surely his judgement couldn't be that skewed?

'You *are* a bastard.' But she flushed because he'd never given her the chance to explain about Eric and it was understandable that he had somehow ended up with the wrong end of the stick. She looked at him, her bright eyes filled with unspoken challenge. 'And how very lucky you are that I won't be hanging around and making a nuisance of myself by demanding anything from you. I'm not the nasty gold-digger you seemed to think I am and I wouldn't touch a penny from you if my life depended on it!'

'You're telling me that you weren't after money from me by trying to encourage me to do a deal with your father? Even though you knew that his company was on the brink of collapse? Even though you knew that he was probably criminally involved in skimming cash from the till?' Matias laughed shortly. 'Let's have your definition of a gold-digger, then, Sophie...'

'I don't care what you think of me,' Sophie said tightly. She'd had her tale to tell, had been ready to spill the beans about Eric because she had been seduced by Matias on an emotional level, had taken him for being someone he had not been. She'd had a narrow escape—so should she spill the beans *now*?

No way, she decided grimly. He was still after

her father and there was no way she would allow Eric's privacy to be invaded by the press, which was exactly what could happen should Matias choose to publicise her brother's existence. Her darling, fragile brother was not going to be part of Matias's retribution or even unintentional *collateral damage.*

Matias instantly realised that that simple statement held the distinct possibility of opening up another quagmire and so he opted for silence.

'So what is your explanation for your behaviour?' he eventually demanded, grudgingly curious to find out what she would be able to come up with that didn't begin and end with her need to have money injected into her company.

'I don't have to provide you with an explanation,' Sophie retorted quickly, cringing back from a vision of reporters banging on the window of her brother's bedroom, terrifying him because he would be hopelessly confused and panicked.

'I just need to take everything you say at face value and believe you. Is that it?'

'You don't have to do anything you don't want

to do. I haven't come here because I want anything from you and there's no *we* in this situation. I came here because I felt it was the right thing to do but this isn't a problem that I'm forcing you to face. I don't trust you, Matias, but you deserved to know about the pregnancy so here I am.'

'We're back to this again. Let's move away from that and focus on the present and the future. And just for your reference, there very much *is* a *we* in this situation because half of my chromosomes, whether you like it or not, happen to be inside you right now in the form of a baby neither of us expected but which both of us have to deal with.' His instinct was to qualify what he had to say by telling her that everything depended on whether she was telling the truth, but he decided that silence on that subject was definitely going to be the diplomatic course. 'You're having my baby…' For a few seconds he was stunned again by the impact that had on him. Matias Rivero, a father. He still couldn't quite get his head round that. 'If you thought that you could just pass on that information and then walk away, job done, then you were sorely mistaken. I won't be walking away from my responsibility, Sophie.'

'I don't want to be your responsibility.'

'You're not but my unborn child is, whether you like it or not. I didn't sign up to this but it's happened and we have to deal with it. You have an unhappy family background so maybe that's led you to imagine that stability is overrated, but I haven't and I am a firm believer in the importance of having parents in a child's life. Both parents.'

'I happen to believe very strongly in stability,' Sophie corrected him tightly, '*because* I've had an unhappy family background. I didn't know how you would react when I came to see you, bearing in mind the way we parted company, but you can rest assured that I won't stand in the way of your seeing your child.' She hated the way he made her feel. She didn't want to be here, and yet, in his presence, she felt so *different*, as though she were living on a plane of heightened sensation. She felt *alive*. She wanted to walk out but felt compelled to stay. She wanted to ignore his staggering, unwelcome impact on her senses but was drawn to him by invisible strings that she couldn't seem to sever. She loathed him for what he had done and loathed herself almost as much for knowing that somewhere inside her he still stirred something...something only he could somehow manage to reach.

'That's not good enough, *querida*.' Matias had never contemplated marriage and now here he was, facing marriage as the final frontier, and not simply marriage, but marriage to the woman who was the daughter of his sworn enemy. And yet what other solution was there? He had no intention of being a bit player in his child's life, forking out maintenance payments while having his visiting rights restricted and curtailed by a vengeful mother. Sophie wouldn't forget the circumstances that had brought him into her life and she would have the perfect opportunity, should she so choose, to wreak a little healthy revenge of her own by dictating how much or how little influence he had over his own flesh and blood.

He thought of his mother, recovering in a private hospital in London. She would be so upset if she ended up as only a part-time grandparent, snatching moments here and there with a grandchild caught in a tug of war between two warring parents. Matias might have been put off emotional commitment thanks to a conniving ex and the lessons learnt from his own emotional father and where it had got him in the long run. That said, he hadn't been lying when he'd told Sophie that his childhood had consisted of a strong and supportive family unit and now, in the face of this unexpected development, that strong family bond locked into place to override everything else.

'Twenty minutes ago, you were telling me that time was money, so I'd better go now.'

'Things change. Twenty minutes ago I didn't realise that you were carrying my baby.' His sharp eyes were glued to her face while he programmed his brain to accept the news she had broken to him, to start thinking outside the box. 'You're now set to be a permanent feature in my life. I want to be there for my child twenty-four-seven and the only way that can be achieved is if we marry.'

Deathly silence greeted this extraordinary statement and Sophie's mouth inelegantly fell open in shock.

'You've got to be kidding.'

'You might have come here out of a sense of duty but I have no intention of going away like an unpleasant smell because you refuse to accept that the past is over and done with.'

'I will never forget how you used me in your quest for revenge. You used me once and who's to say that you won't use me again?' She thought of Eric, the secret that Matias could not be allowed to uncover because what if his desire for revenge hadn't been sated? She looked at him from under lowered lashes and shivered. So beautiful, so powerful and so incredibly ruthless.

'Sophie, that story has ended. We are travelling down a different road now.' But Matias was genuinely puzzled by her statement. What else could he possibly use her for? For better or for worse, he had uncovered everything there was to uncover about her father.

He continued to look at her and noted the way her cheeks slowly coloured, arrowed in on the soft tremble of her full lips. The air between them was suddenly filled with a charge he recognised all too well, a sexual charge that made him immediately harden for her. He vividly recalled the silky wetness that always greeted his exploring fingers, his questing mouth, and he clenched his jaw.

He motioned, without looking around, for the bill and wondered whether she was conscious of the signals she was sending out under all the hostility and mistrust, signals that were as powerful as a deep sea-depth charge, signals that advertised a connection between them that was founded on the oldest thing in the world…sexual attraction.

'Think about it, Sophie, and I will call you tomorrow so that we can pick up this conversation.' He smiled slowly and watched intently as a little shiver went through her. 'I think we both need to do a little private reflection, don't you?'

CHAPTER EIGHT

SHE'D TURNED DOWN his extraordinary marriage proposal and she'd done the right thing.

Of course there were pros and there were cons. Every decision was always laced with pros and cons! But she had done the right thing. She'd been to see Eric, sat in his soothing presence, watched his contentment in his peaceful surroundings. Somehow she'd find the money to pay for him carrying on living there, but she would never expose him to the cruel glare of a curious and judgemental public.

Was she being selfish? Was she failing to consider the reality, which was that a child would always be better off with two parents as opposed to one and that was something that should override every other concern?

No. How could you hitch your wagon to a man you didn't trust? A man you felt might betray you again? And anyway, trust issues aside, two parents only worked if the glue that bound them together wasn't a child, but love. Matias didn't love her and he had never pretended that he did. He felt responsible for her, responsible for the child he had sired, and was admirably willing to step up to the plate and do his duty, but duty was a far cry from love.

Duty would wear very thin at the edges as time marched on. Duty would be the very thing he would come to resent when he found himself harnessed to a woman he would never have voluntarily chosen to spend his life with.

But three weeks had gone by and Matias just seemed to *be around so much*.

He hadn't said it in so many words, but there had been no need because every look he gave her and every word that passed his lips said *don't fight me*.

She'd turned him down but, like a predator waiting for the right moment to strike, he was simply biding his time.

He didn't realise, she thought, that he would never wear away her defences because there was more than just her and their baby at stake. At stake was a brother he knew nothing about and never would and that bolstered all her resolve when his presence just felt *too overwhelming*.

Nothing he could say, no logic he could use, could ever make her do anything that might jeopardise her brother's privacy and happiness.

She was congratulating herself on being strong as she sat, the first to arrive, at the posh restaurant where Matias had arranged to meet her for lunch. He had been away for the past three days and her stomach was already tightening in nervous knots as she braced herself for that first glimpse of him. On the one hand, she had been relieved that, although he had been scrupulous about maintaining contact with her by phone, he hadn't imposed his presence on her on a daily basis. On the other hand, she wondered whether she might have become more blasé about his physical presence if he were around more, if she had a chance to get accustomed to him. She didn't like the way he still made her feel and she hated the memories of him touching her that refused to go away. They weren't on that page any longer! Things had changed and they were never going to be on that page together again.

Lost in thought, she looked up to find that he had arrived and he wasn't alone.

Art was with him. She hadn't seen him since the weekend party in the Lake District and she rose to her feet, already smiling as he walked towards her. Behind him, Matias towered, unbearably sexy in his work clothes, one hand in his trouser pocket, the other hooked to his jacket, which was slung over his shoulder.

Seeing that warm, genuine smile on her face as she looked at Art, Matias sourly thought that it was something *he* hadn't seen for a while. She'd repeatedly thrown his marriage proposals back in his face and he'd been sharp enough to realise that the harder he pushed, the faster she would back away.

There was no way he was going to let her run out of his life because it suited her. Pride refused to let him forget that she had slept with him as a ruse to get him to invest in her father's company, but common sense dictated that he get her onside because he was never going to be persuaded into the role of part-time father.

He watched, his expression shuttered, as she and Art chatted away like the old friends they weren't and something hit him hard, something so unexpected that it was like a punch to the gut.

He didn't like seeing her relaxed interaction with his friend. He didn't like the way she was so at ease in his company. He didn't care for the tinkling of her laughter as they found God only knew what to talk about, considering they'd known each other all of five seconds.

Jealousy and possessiveness rammed into him with the weight of a sledgehammer and he interrupted their conversation to coolly inform her that Art wasn't going to be joining them for lunch.

'That's a shame.' Sophie sighed with genuine disappointment, which got on Matias's nerves even more.

He scowled, met Art's curious eyes and scowled even more. 'Don't let us keep you,' he said abruptly, and Art grinned broadly but stood up, moving to drop a kiss on Sophie's cheek before heading out.

'That was *so* rude,' she said. 'It was lovely seeing Art again! I had no idea you two were so close. You never said! I can't believe you *grew up together*!' They were like brothers and it had brought her up short to acknowledge that Art adored Matias. Even in the space of half an hour, she had been able to glean that from their interaction and seeing them together had unwillingly reminded her of just why she had been seduced by him. There was a side to Matias that wasn't a bastard, a side that could elicit a depth of affection from a loyal friend who was clearly a wonderful human being. It was suddenly confusing to admit that he was also many other things, a complex guy with so many dimensions, it made her head swim.

Not that she was going to let that deflect her from the path she had decided to take.

'I had no idea I had a duty to tell you every detail of my life just because you're carrying my baby,' Matias drawled lazily, sitting back as menus were placed in front of them. Her cheeks were still flushed and she looked so damned sexy that the jealousy that had attacked him from nowhere five minutes ago staged another onslaught. He knew he was being irrational but he couldn't help it.

'You never said that you were going to visit your mother...'

'I could hardly let her find out about us via the grapevine.'

'She must have been disappointed,' Sophie said quietly. 'No mother likes to think that her child has...well...is going to have a family...you know...so unexpectedly...and without the usual build-up...'

Matias allowed her to run aground. Seeing his mother had reinforced his belief that the only solution was to marry the woman blushing opposite him. If she was going to dig her heels in, then he would have to work along the lines that there was more than one way to skin a cat. He'd seen the way she still looked at him. 'Naturally,' he murmured smoothly, 'she would have preferred the love and marriage scenario...'

'But you told her how it was? That this isn't that sort of situation?'

Matias didn't say anything because he had told his mother no such thing. 'Pregnancy becomes you, Sophie,' he said instead, relaxing into the chair and staring at her until the faint colour in her cheeks deepened and he saw the latent *awareness* of him that she was always so careful to try and conceal. 'Your body's changing. You're wearing looser clothes. Are your breasts getting bigger?'

'Matias!' Sophie was shocked because he hadn't been direct like this before.

Heat blossomed inside her. Her breasts ached and she felt the tingle of awareness stickily making its presence felt between her legs. *That* was what those casual words were doing to her!

'It doesn't get more intimate than having my baby...' he shrugged, his fabulous eyes not leaving her face '...so why are you so surprised that I am curious about the physical changes occurring to you? It's natural. I'm fifty per cent responsible for those physical changes.'

'This conversation is not appropriate! We no longer have that kind of relationship!'

'You think that we are more like…*what*?'

'Well, *friends*. At least, that's what we should be aspiring to become! We've talked about this and we both agree that it would be best for our child if we remain on good terms.' She cleared her throat and tried to ignore the suffocating effect his intense gaze was having on her nervous system. 'Remember we agreed that you would be able to see him or her any time you wanted?'

'So we did…'

'We may not have expected this…' she dug deep to repeat the mantra she had told herself '…but we're both adults and um…in this day and age, marriage isn't the inevitable solution to dealing with an unexpected pregnancy… We discussed this.'

'Indeed…'

'There's too much water under the bridge between us.'

'I won't deny that.' She had deferred, for once, and he had ordered for both of them, a sharing platter that was now placed between them. 'But

I'm curious. What do you suggest we do with the mutual desire that's still putting in an unwelcome appearance?'

Sophie's mouth fell open. He had brought out into the open the one thing she had desperately tried to shove into a locked box. 'I don't know what you're talking about!'

'Liar,' Matias said softly. 'I could reach out and touch you right now and you'd go up in flames.'

'You couldn't be further from the truth,' Sophie denied weakly. 'I could never be attracted to someone who used me like you did. Never!'

'*Never* is a word that has no place in my vocabulary.'

'Matias…' She thought of Eric and the importance of hanging onto her resolve, but seeing Matias with Art had weakened that resolve, had reminded her of those sides to him that could be so wonderfully seductive, so thoughtful and unexpectedly kind.

'I'm listening.'

'I know you find it funny to make me uncomfortable.'

'I think about you all the time. I wonder what

your changing body looks like under those clothes.'

'Don't say things like that! We don't have that kind of relationship! We talked about that.' She sought refuge in the platter in front of her but she could feel him staring lazily at her, sending her into heady meltdown. Her whole body was throbbing with the very awareness he was casually dragging out into the open and forcing her to acknowledge.

'I don't like to stick to the script. It makes for a boring life.' Matias sat back. He let his eyes drift at a leisurely pace down her curvaceous body and felt his mouth twitch because she was as rigid as a plank of wood, as if her posture were fooling him. 'In fact,' he drawled, 'I'm taking the afternoon off.'

'Why?'

'Do I have to provide a reason? And stop looking at me like that. You should be thrilled at the prospect of spending time in my company. And do me a favour and refrain from telling me that we *don't have that kind of relationship.*'

'I can't leave Julie in the lurch.'

'She's going to have to get used to you no longer holding her hand when you finally decide to listen to me and quit working. She's a big girl. She'll cope.'

'I can't *quit working*, Matias.'

'Let's not go there. You don't need the money.'

Sophie thought of Eric and her mouth firmed. The irony was that Matias wanted to throw money at her. Once upon a time not all that long ago he had turned his back on her and tossed her to the kerb but now that she was pregnant, everything had changed. They had not discussed money in any great depth yet, but he had already made it clear that his child, and her by extension, would want for nothing.

And yet, how could she allow herself to ever become financially dependent on him? Her pride would never allow it and, more than that, what if she began to trust again only to find that she had once more made a mistake? What if, by then, she was totally reliant on the money he was so keen for her to have because she'd stopped working? No, there was no way she could give up her job.

Maternity leave was one thing. Resignation was quite another.

Another roadblock, Matias thought with frustration. He impatiently wondered why she couldn't just recognise that his solution was the best and only way to move forward. What woman wouldn't want a life of luxury? What woman wouldn't want to be able to snap her fingers and get whatever she wanted? It wasn't as though they didn't have an electric connection still thrumming between them like a live charge. What more advantages did he have to bring to the table for her to accept his proposal? Why, he thought, did she have to be so *damned stubborn*?

'I've taken the afternoon off, *querida*, because I have a surprise for you.'

'I hate surprises,' Sophie confessed.

'I know. I'm not a big fan of them myself but I am hoping you'll like this one. It's a house.'

'A house?'

'For you,' he said bluntly and her eyes widened in surprise.

'You've gone and bought a house *for me*?' She bristled. 'Why would you do that?'

Matias sat back, taking his own sweet time, and looked at her evenly. 'Because,' he said calmly, 'you won't be bringing up our child in that tiny box of yours with its converted kitchen.'

'There's nothing wrong with *that box*,' Sophie cried hotly as pride kicked in and lodged inside her.

'Don't argue with me on this.' Matias's voice was forbidding. 'You've turned down my marriage proposal, in defiance of common sense. You've dug your heels in and dismissed all financial help I've offered as unnecessary handouts. You've insisted on working long hours even though you're unnecessarily putting our child at risk. You are *not* going to wage war with me on this.'

'How have I been putting the baby at risk?' Sophie asked furiously.

'You don't have to work until midnight baking cakes for anyone's anniversary party.'

'*Once.* I've done that *once*!'

'Or,' Matias ploughed on remorselessly, 'waste three hours in traffic delivering a four-course meal for a dinner party.'

'That's my job!'

'You're overexerting yourself. You need to take it easy.'

Sophie released a long sigh but… *Had any-one ever really looked out for her? Ever really cared whether she was taking on too much or not?* Of course, this wasn't about *her*, but about the precious cargo in her stomach, and it would be downright foolhardy to start thinking otherwise *but still…*

'I know you're not a gold-digger, Sophie. You don't have to keep trying to prove it to me over and over again.'

'That's not what I'm doing.'

'No? Then what is it?'

'I won't rely on you financially. I can't. I need to have my own financial independence.' Suddenly she felt small and helpless. She wished she were able to lean on him and just accept what was on offer. He made it sound so easy. Clean break from what had happened between them in the past and onward bound to the future he wanted her and his child to have, but there was so much more to the story than he knew.

'Well, you're going to have to compromise on this, whether you like it or not, *cara*.' His voice was cool and unyielding.

Their eyes tangled. He reached out and brushed a speck of something from the side of her mouth, then left his finger there for a few seconds to stroke it over her lips. 'A little bread,' he said roughly, his big body firing up immediately because it was the first time he'd touched her in weeks.

Sophie's eyes widened. For a minute there she had leaned towards him and her whole body had burned from the inside out, as though molten lava were running through her veins. *The way he was looking at her, with those deep, dark, sexy eyes...*

Yearning made her weak and it was a struggle to pull away from the magnetic drag on her senses.

'You have no idea what my taste is like. In houses.' Which was as good as accepting whatever over-the-top house he had flung money at, in defiance of the fact that he must have known that she would have kicked up a fuss about it. Her heart was still hammering and she lowered her eyes and took a few deep breaths before looking at him once again. She could still feel the burning of her skin where he had touched her. 'Don't get me wrong, Matias.' Her tone crisped up but her body, awakened by his touch, *wanted more*. 'You have a lovely place in the Lake District but I couldn't imagine living in a massive greenhouse like that. I don't know what your apartment's like but I'm guessing it's along the same lines...'

'Damned by faint praise,' Matias murmured, wanting her more than he had ever wanted anything or anyone in his life before and damn well determined to have her because he could *smell* the same want radiating from her in waves.

'What I'm saying is you and I obviously don't have the same taste in houses so it's unlikely I'm going to like whatever it is you've bought.'

'I haven't bought it yet,' he drawled. 'I may be arrogant but I thought you might actually like to have a say in the house you want to live in.' Eyes on her, he signalled for the bill and then stood up.

He dominated the space around him and she was helplessly drawn towards him, like a moth to a bright light. She couldn't quite understand how it was that he could continue to exercise this powerful effect on her after what he had done, or how common sense and logic hadn't prevailed when it came to stepping back from him. She wondered whether pregnancy hormones had taken over and were controlling all her responses, heightening her emotional state and making her vulnerable to him when she should have been as detached from him as he was from her and getting down to the business of building a friendship for the sake of the child she was carrying.

Outside, his chauffeur was waiting for them, but instead of accompanying them he drove them to his office where they switched cars, and Matias took the wheel.

'Where is this house?' Sophie asked because she had expected something in Chelsea or Mayfair or one of those frighteningly expensive postcodes close to where he had his own apartment.

'I'm going to disappoint you...' he slid his

eyes sideways to glance at her and smiled '...by keeping it a surprise. Now, talk to me, *querida*. Don't argue with me. Tell me about that client of yours...'

'Which client?' Because stupidly, even though she had so many defences erected when it came to Matias you could construct a small town behind them, she *still* found it frighteningly easy to talk to him when he turned on that charm of his.

'The vegan with the wart on her face.'

'I didn't think I'd mentioned her to you.'

'When we're not fighting,' Matias murmured softly, 'we're getting along a hell of a lot better than you give us credit for. There's so much more we could be doing, *querida*, instead of making war...'

Sophie only realised that they had been driving for longer than she thought when the crowded streets and houses fell away to open space and parks and they pulled up outside a picture-perfect house shaped like a chocolate box with an extension to one side. Wisteria clambered over the front wall and, set right back from the lane, the front garden was dilapidated and overgrown.

'It needs work,' Matias told her, reaching into the pocket of his jacket, which he had flung in the back seat, and extracting some keys, which he jangled on one finger as he opened his car door. 'And it hasn't been lived in for several months, hence the exuberance of the weeds.'

'I hadn't expected anything like this.' Sophie followed him up to the front door, head swinging left to right as she looked around her. The house stood in its own small plot, which was hedged in on three sides. He opened the door, stood aside and she brushed past him and then stood and stared.

There were rooms to the right and left of the hallway. Lovely square rooms, all perfectly proportioned. A sitting room, a more formal living room, a study, a snug and then along to the kitchen and conservatory, which opened out at the back to a garden that was full of trees and shrubs and plants that had taken advantage of absentee owners and decided to run rampant.

The paint was faded. In the sitting room, the

gently flowered wallpaper seemed to speak of a different era.

'The house was owned by an elderly lady who lived here for most of her life, it would seem,' Matias was murmuring as he led her from room to room. 'She didn't have any children, or perhaps they might have persuaded her that the house was far too big as she got older, but it would seem that she was too attached to it to sell up and leave and as a consequence the latter part of her life was spent in only a handful of rooms. The rest were left in a state of gradual decline. When she died a little over a year ago, it was inherited by a distant relative abroad and the probate took some time, hence it's only just come onto the market.'

She walked from room to room. Her silence spoke volumes. She wasn't bristling; she wasn't complaining. In the matter of the house, he had clearly won hands down.

Matias intended to win hands down in every other area as well.

He was waiting for her in the hallway, leaning against the wall, when she completed her third tour of the house, and he didn't budge as she walked towards him, her eyes still wide as saucers.

'Okay.' Sophie smiled crookedly. 'You win.'

'I know.'

'Don't be arrogant, Matias,' but she was still smiling and she wasn't trying to shuffle more distance between them. The silence stretched until she licked her lips nervously.

But she hadn't taken flight.

'I don't just want to win when it comes to finding a house for…you,' he said gruffly.

'Matias, don't.' But her voice was high and unsteady, and against her will her body was straining with desperate longing towards him, liquid pooling between her legs, the swollen tips of her nipples tightening into sensitive buds.

'Why do you insist on fighting this thing that's still here between us?'

'Because we can't give in to…to lust…'

'So you finally admit it.'

'That doesn't mean anything. It doesn't mean I'm going to do anything about it.' She looked at him and couldn't look away. His dark eyes pinned her to the spot with ruthless efficiency. She couldn't move, couldn't think, could scarcely breathe.

Her head screamed that this was *just not going to do*. She couldn't afford to lose sight of what was sensible but her body was singing from a different song sheet and when he lowered his head to hers, her hands reached out. To push him away? Maybe. Yet they didn't. They curled into his shirt and she melted helplessly as he kissed her, softly and teasingly at first and then with a hunger that matched her own.

His tongue found hers. His hands, on her shoulders, moved to her arms then cupped the full weight of her breasts.

He played with her nipples through her top but then, frustrated, pushed open the buttons and groaned as he felt the naked skin of her chest and then, burrowing beneath the lacy bra, finally got to the silky fullness of her breasts and the ripe protrusion of a nipple.

'You're definitely bigger.' His voice was shaking.

'Matias...'

'Touch me.' He guided her hand to his erection, which was a hard, prominent bulge against the zipper of his trousers.

'We can't make love here!'

Wrenched back to the reality of what she was saying, Matias struggled not to explode in his trousers. He breathed deeply, cupped the nape of her neck and drew her to him so that their foreheads were touching.

Her breath was minty fresh, her skin as soft as satin and he ached for her. 'We talk, Sophie,' he breathed in a driven undertone. 'Don't tell me we're at one another's throats all of the time. And we want one another.'

Sophie knew what he was saying and she longed to capitulate but she was only in this place because she was pregnant. Had she not been, they would be enemies on opposite sides of the fence. Were it just a question of her, then would she think about his offer? Maybe. She could cope if it turned out that she couldn't trust him. Again. But she couldn't trust him with Eric. Could she?

Confusion tore through her.

'Come back to my place with me,' he urged.

'I won't marry you,' she said weakly.

Matias all but groaned in frustration but he didn't. Instead, he smoothed his hands over her shoulders and kissed her very gently, very persuasively on her mouth and felt her move from hesitation to abandon. He kept kissing her. He kissed her until she was breathless. He kissed her until he knew for certain that there was nothing and no one left in her head but him, then he broke apart and said, in a barely restrained voice,

'Let's go.'

CHAPTER NINE

HER HOUSE.

In her head, to go to Matias's house would have been a complete declaration of defeat. Within the confines of her own four walls, however, she could kid herself that she was still in control, even though she had lost it in his arms and even though *she wanted to carry on losing it.*

If I sleep with him, she thought, then it would be *a conscious decision.* It wouldn't mean that she had lost all control and it certainly didn't mean that she would marry him. She would never trust him again. How could she? She would never jeopardise Eric's privacy because she'd made another mistake, but…

She wanted Matias so badly. He was in her system like a virus and she wanted to be cleared of that virus because it was driving her round the bend.

He reached out to link his fingers lightly through hers in the car. They barely spoke but the electricity between them could have set a forest ablaze. His mobile phone rang several times. He ignored it. Looking at his strong, sharp profile, the lean contours of his beautiful face, Sophie wondered what was going through his head. He didn't love her but he still fancied her. He'd told her that there was no need for her to keep trying to prove to him that she was no gold-digger, but deep down she knew that he would always believe her culpable of trying to get him to sink money into her father's dying company and invest in a man who had turned out to be a thief. He had no idea that Eric existed and so would never understand why she had done what she had, and she could never tell him about her brother because family loyalty was more powerful than anything else.

But whatever the situation, he was right. A fire burned between them and what were they to do about it?

Having never invested in the crazy notion that lust was something that couldn't be tamed, Sophie was realising just how far off the mark she'd been with her orderly, smug little homilies.

It was after four-thirty by the time they made it to her house. Sophie thought it was serendipity that Julie was out on a job, setting up with an assistant they had hired, for a lavish dinner party in Dulwich.

Compared to the glorious setting of the house they had just seen, her two up, two down, squashed in the middle of an uninspiring row of terraced lookalikes, was a shock to the system. She'd vigorously defended her little place but now she felt that she could see it through Matias's eyes. Poky, cramped, unsatisfactory.

She turned to find him looking at her with a veiled expression as he quietly shut the door behind them. Shivers of anticipation raced up and down her spine.

'Empty house?' he asked, walking very slowly towards her, and Sophie nodded.

'Julie's on a job. She won't be back until tomorrow afternoon. Matias... I'm glad about the house... This place would really not have been suitable for a baby. I mean, of course, it would have worked if there were no other option but...'

'Shh.' He placed one finger over her lips and her heart sped up. 'Don't talk.' He was directly in front of her now and he bent his head and kissed her. A long, lingering, gentle kiss that made her weak at the knees. 'Much as I enjoy the sound of you telling me that I was right, there's more, a lot more, I want to enjoy right now.' He cupped the back of her neck and carried on kissing her, taking it long and slow and feeling a kick of satisfaction as her body yielded to his, moulding bit by bit to his hard length until they were pressed together, entwined.

Without warning, he lifted her off her feet and Sophie gasped and clung to him as he made his way up the narrow staircase.

He'd seen enough of her place to know that finding her bedroom wasn't going to require in-depth navigation skills. The place was tiny. He doubted there were more than two bedrooms and he was proved right, finding hers with no trouble at all as it was at the top of the stairs.

Cheerful colours tried to make the most of a

space that could barely contain the bed, the chest of drawers and the wardrobe that were crammed into it. Two posters tried to attract the eye away from the view outside of other terraced houses and beyond that a railway line.

He set her down on the bed and she promptly pushed herself up onto her elbows to look at him as he drew the curtains together, shutting out the weak sunlight and plunging the room into subdued tones of grey and sepia.

'It's been too long,' he intoned with a slow, possessive smile that ratcheted up her spiralling excitement.

He was standing with his back to the window and he remained there for a few seconds, just staring at her, before walking towards the bed, ridding himself of clothes on the way.

He was sheer masculine, powerful beauty in motion and he took her breath away.

She was frankly amazed that she had been able to withstand his potent sex appeal for as long as she had, but then today was the first time he had yanked that monster out of the cupboard and forced her to confront it.

She half closed her eyes, watching as, down to his boxers, he stood by the side of the bed and gazed down at her.

Tentatively, she reached out and ran the tips of her fingers across the washboard hardness of his flat stomach.

He was wired for her. His erection was prominent under the boxers, which didn't remain on for longer than necessary.

'I don't have to tell you how much I want this,' Matias said gruffly. 'The evidence is right in front of you.'

Sophie gave a soft little whimper and sat up straighter, angling her body so that she could lick the shaft of his pulsing erection.

She tasted him like someone savouring an exquisite delicacy. Her tongue flicked and touched, her mouth closed over him and she sucked while, with her hand, she enjoyed the familiar feel of his hardness. His taste was an aphrodisiac.

She felt as if somewhere, in the back of her mind, she had stored the memory of the noises he made when she did this, his deep, guttural grunts. His fingers clasped in her hair were familiar. She wanted him so badly she was melting for him and wanted nothing more than to fling off all her clothes so that he could take her.

Reading her mind and knowing that if he didn't watch it, he would come right now, in her mouth, Matias reluctantly separated her from him. When he glanced down, his shaft was slick and wet and he had to clench his fists to control the urge to put her right back there, have her take him across the finishing line with her hands and her mouth.

No. He'd fantasised about this for far too long to blow it on a horny, teenage urge to grab and take.

But hell, he was on fire as he sank onto the mattress so that he could remove her clothes.

She was wearing far too much and he was way too fired up to do justice to the striptease scenario. He needed to get under the layers of fabric as quickly as possible so that he could feel her.

Her clothes hit the deck in record time and she helped, squirming out of her cumbersome bra and wriggling free of the lacy underwear, which, he noted in passing satisfaction, was of the sexy thong variety, a choice of lingerie he knew he had encouraged her to wear.

It was almost a shame that he was so hot and hard because he would have liked to have taken his time teasing her with his tongue through the lace of her underwear.

'Matias…' Sophie fell back against the pillow and arched a little so that her full breasts were pushed out invitingly to him.

He was kneeling over her and, on cue, he took her breasts in his big hands and massaged them gently until his thumbs were grazing her nipples and sending shivers of racing pleasure straight downwards.

She circled him with her hand and played with him, knowing just how fast and firm he liked the rhythmic motion of her hand.

'Matias…what?' he encouraged with a wicked smile and she looked back at him with wry understanding because she knew just what he wanted.

'You know…' she blushed furiously '…what I like…'

'Oh, I know…' He bent to suckle her nipple,

drawing it into his mouth and taking his time to lave it with his tongue, circling the aching tip until she was writhing under him.

He knew her so well. It felt as though they had been making love for ever. Knew that she liked him to be just a little rough, to nip her big, pouting nipples until she became even wetter and more restless. He knew what else she loved, and he explored lower down her glorious body, taking time to appreciate all the small changes he had wondered about.

Her breasts were at least a cup size bigger and her nipples were more pronounced in colour, no longer a rosy blush but a deeper hue. Her belly was just a bit more rounded. Having never thought about babies or becoming a father, at least not since the hapless incident a thousand years ago with the ex-girlfriend who had tried it on, he had never looked twice at pregnant women, but this woman, with his baby inside her, was beyond sexy.

Her roundness thrilled him, made him even harder than he already was.

Working his way down her body, he slipped his

hand between her legs and played with the soft down between them. Then he slipped his finger into her and she moaned softly and squirmed until his finger was deeper inside her, finding her softness and working a path to the tiny bud that was begging for attention.

He knew that if he dawdled too long there, she would come. She was the most responsive woman he had ever known. So he played with the tingling bud, then stopped, then played with it again, until she was begging him to take her.

'Not just yet,' he whispered. Hands on her waist, he dropped down between her legs and nuzzled, breathing in her honeyed sweetness.

He flicked his tongue along the slit of her womanhood, then began exploring her wetness.

His finger had already teased her and now his tongue did the teasing, until she was moaning and wriggling, pushing him down hard one minute, jerking him up the next, her fingers curled into his hair.

She bucked against his mouth, rising up with jerky movements, and he cupped her buttocks, holding her still and torturing her with the insistent push of his tongue inside her.

'I'm going to come,' she gasped as her body began moving quicker to capture every small sensation of him between her legs. 'I don't want to come like this, Matias... I want to *feel you inside me.*'

Matias rose up. He automatically reached down to find his wallet but then he remembered that there was no need for protection and he dealt her a slashing smile.

'The horse has already bolted...' he grinned '...so no need to do anything about locking the stable door.'

Sophie drowsily returned his smile. Her body was hot and flushed and the waves of pleasure that had almost but not quite taken her over the edge were still there, making her want to wriggle and touch herself.

'You're so hot for me, *querida...*'

'I can't help it,' Sophie half groaned. 'It's a physical thing.'

'Now, now, don't go spoiling the mood. I want to ride you and take you to the outer reaches of the universe.' He prodded her with the blunt head of his shaft and she parted her legs, unable to contain her eagerness to have him deep inside her.

He slid in and the sensation was beyond belief. She was slick and wet and tight and her softness welcomed him in ways that he couldn't define but just knew made him feel better than good.

He wanted her so badly. This was going to have to be fast and hard. He couldn't hang around any longer, he couldn't devote any more time to foreplay or else he risked the unthinkable.

He drove into her, thrusting long and deep, and she wrapped her legs around his waist and, yes, he rode her until she was bucking and crying out with pleasure, until the breathing hitched in her throat. Until, cresting a wave, she came just as he did, with a rush of sensation that flowed over her and around her like a tsunami.

She arched up and stiffened as his powerful body shuddered against her and she panted and rocked beneath him until at last…she was spent.

Matias levered himself off her. It was a downright miracle of circumstance that he now found himself here, with her. The number of *what ifs* between them could have stocked a library.

What if…she hadn't crashed into his car?

What if…he hadn't lived a life hell-bent on revenge?

What if…he hadn't seen fit to weave her into his revenge agenda?

What if…she hadn't spent time under his roof at his place in the Lake District?

What if, what if, what if…?

But here they were, having made the most satisfying love imaginable. In no way, shape or form was he tiring of her. On the contrary, he desired her with an urgency that none of his other relationships had ever had. He felt a possessiveness towards her that defied belief.

He had accepted the shock to his system that impending and unforeseen fatherhood would confer.

He had risen above the challenge of playing a blame game that would get neither of them anywhere.

But had he really believed that this unforeseeable passion and downright *insatiable craving* would form a part of the picture? Was it the evidence of his own virility and the fact that she was carrying his baby that made his feelings towards her so...*ferociously powerful*?

She had stuck to her guns about not marrying him, frustrating his natural urge to get what he wanted. His powerful need to *never* back down until he had what should be his within his grasp had hit a roadblock with her. He refused to contemplate any situation that involved him losing control over his child, and by extension, he told himself, *her*.

Seeing his mother as she recuperated in hospital, as he had now done several times, had only reinforced his determination to take her as his wife.

Thus far, the inevitable meeting between his mother and Sophie had been avoided, but sooner or later his mother would want to meet the woman who was carrying her grandchild and when that time arrived Matias was determined that marriage would be on the cards. There would be no difficult conversation in which his mother would be forced to concede that the grandchild she had always longed for would be a fleeting presence in her life.

'Was that as good for you as it was for me, *querida*?' He shifted onto his side and manoeuvred her so that they were facing one another. He brushed a strand of hair away from her face and then kissed her very gently on her mouth, tracing the outline of her lips with his tongue.

Sophie struggled to think straight. She had done what she had spent weeks resolving not to do. She had climbed back into bed with him and where did that leave the *friendship* angle she had been working so hard at since she had turned down his marriage proposal?

What disturbed and alarmed her was the fact that it had felt *right*.

Because…because…

Because she loved him. Because he'd swept into her life, inappropriate and infuriatingly arrogant, and stolen her heart, and even though he had used her and couldn't be trusted, because who knew whether he would use her again, she still couldn't help but love him. She'd made love to him and it had been as wonderful and as satisfying as walking through the front door of the house you adored and finding safety within its four walls. Which was a joke, of course, but then so were all the stupid assumptions she had made about love being something she would have been able to control. She could no more have controlled what she felt for Matias than she could have controlled the direction of a hurricane.

'Well?' Matias prompted, curving a hand possessively around her waist, challenging her to deny what was glaringly obvious.

'It was nice,' Sophie said faintly, still wrapped in the revelation that had been lurking there, just below the surface, for longer than she cared to think.

'Nice? *Nice?*' Matias was tempted to explode with outrage but ended up bursting out laughing. 'You certainly know how to shoot a man down in flames.'

'Okay.' She blushed. 'It was pretty good.'

'Getting better,' he mused, 'but I still prefer *amazing*.'

'It was amazing.'

'When you showed up at my office,' Matias

said softly, 'it was a shock, but I really want this baby, *querida*. You tell me you don't want to marry me. You tell me the ingredients for a successful marriage aren't in place, but we talk. Yes, we fight as well, but *we talk*. And we still have this thing between us. We still want one another passionately. Isn't that glue enough? You say you're not prepared to make sacrifices yet *I* am, because I truly feel that any sacrifice I make for the sake of our child will, in the end, be worth it. Don't we both want what, ultimately, will be best for our baby? Can you deny that? We can't change the past but we can move on from it. We can stop it from altering the course of the future.'

Sophie could feel the pulse in her neck beating, matching the steady beat of her heart, the heart that belonged to him, to a man who would never, *could* never return the favour.

He talked about sacrifices, though, and surely, *surely* he would never use her again? Not when they shared a child? Could she trust him or had the past damaged that irreparably?

'Maybe you're right,' she said, meeting his

eyes steadily. 'Of course I want what's best for our baby. Of course I know that two parents are always going to be better than one.' And maybe, she dared to hope, in time she would trust him enough to confide in him about her brother, despite what had happened between them. Alan had turned away from what he had perceived as a challenge too far in Eric and she had locked herself away after that. Of course, she had never consciously decided that remaining on her own was the preferred option, but how could any relationship ever have blossomed in the bitterness that had grown over the hope and trust she had invested in her ex-boyfriend? Alan had not deserved the faith she had put in him. Compared to Matias, what she'd felt for Alan was a pale shadow of the real thing. But however strong her love, she still couldn't guarantee that Matias, a guy who had been motivated by revenge when he had decided to *cultivate her*, would live up to her expectations.

But they were having a baby together and she *wanted and needed him*.

In due course, he might even jump through all

the hoops and prove to be worthy of her trust, but that was something she would never find out unless she gave him a fighting chance.

Matias looked at her and wished that he could see what she was thinking so seriously about. She was staring back at him but her thoughts were somewhere else. Where? Never had the urge been so strong to *know* someone, completely, utterly and inside out. He had never delved into what the women he dated thought about anything. He had wined and dined them and enjoyed them but digging deep hadn't been part of the equation. Sophie made him want to dig deep.

'So...?' he murmured, with a shuttered expression.

'So we don't have to get married...' Sophie breathed in deep and prayed that she was doing the right thing '...but we can live together...' That was called giving him a chance, giving him an opportunity to prove that he could once more be trusted before she opened up that part of her he knew nothing about.

Matias greeted this with a lot more equanimity

than he felt. Live together? It wasn't the solution he was after, but it would have to do. For now…

Matias got the call as he was about to leave work.

'I'm sorry.' Sophie was obviously moving in a rush. Her voice was tight and panicked. 'I'm going to have to cancel our dinner date tonight. Something's come up, I'm afraid.'

'What's come up?' Already heading to his jacket, which was slung over the back of the cream sofa that occupied the adjoining mini suite in his glasshouse office, Matias paused, returned to the desk and grabbed the little box containing the diamond bracelet he had ordered three days previously and had collected that day as a surprise for her.

He had taken to surprising her every so often with something little, something he had seen somewhere that had reminded him of her.

Once, it had been an antique book on culinary art in Victorian times, which he had quite accidentally found while walking to his car after a meeting on the South Bank. The bookshop had been tucked away next to a small art gallery and he had paused to glance at the offerings in painted crates on trestle tables outside.

She had smiled when he'd given it to her and that smile of genuine pleasure had been worth its weight in gold.

Then he had bought her a set of saucepans specially made for the stove in the new house, because he had found one of her house magazines lying on the sofa with the page creased with an advertisement on their lifetime guarantee and special heat-conducting values. Whatever that was supposed to mean.

And again, that had hit the spot.

The diamond bracelet was the most expensive item he had bought thus far and he sincerely hoped that she wouldn't refuse to accept it. She could dig her heels in and be mulishly stubborn about things that were beyond his comprehension and for reasons he found difficult to fathom.

Matias knew that he was shamelessly directing all his energies into getting what he wanted because the longer he was with her, the more unthinkable it was that she might eventually want to cut short their *living together to see how it goes* status and return to the freedom of single-dom, free to find her soul mate.

He shoved the box into the inside pocket of his jacket, which he had stuck on without breaking the phone connection.

Her voice, the strained tenor of it, was sending alarm bells ringing in his head. She had been fine when he had seen her the day before. They had met for breakfast because she had gone to help Julie and he had wanted to see her before he headed off to Edinburgh, where he was taking a chance on a small pharmaceutical company that was up for grabs.

'Where are you, *querida*?' he asked, doing his utmost to keep his voice calm and composed.

'Matias, I really have to go. The taxi is going to be here any minute and I have to get a few things together before I leave. In fact…wait… the taxi's here.'

'Taxi? Don't you dare hang up on me in the middle of this conversation, Sophie! What taxi? Why are you taking a taxi somewhere? What's wrong with the car? Is it giving you trouble? And where are you going, anyway?'

'The car is fine. I just thought that, in this instance...'

Her voice faded, as though she had dumped the phone on a table because she needed to do something.

What?

Matias was finding it impossible to hang onto his self-control. She sounded as though she was on the verge of tears and Sophie never cried. She had once told him that when things got tough, and there had been plenty of times in her life when they had, then blubbing never solved anything.

It had been just one more thing he had lodged at the back of his mind, something else that slotted into the complex puzzle that comprised her personality.

And now she was on the verge of tears for reasons she would not identify and she didn't want to talk to him about it. He had done his damnedest to prove to her that she had been right to take a punt on him. He had not batted an eyelid at the very clear nesting instincts that had emerged when she had begun decorating the house. He had also gone light on her creep of a father in the wake of the company takeover, allowing him to salvage some measure of self-respect by not sending him to prison for being trigger-happy with the pension pot, although Carney was much diminished by the end of proceedings, which had afforded Matias a great deal of satisfaction.

He had even deflected an immediate visit to see his mother, because, while she was recovering nicely, much spurred on by news of a grandchild on the way, he had wanted to protect Sophie from the inevitable pressing questions about marriage. The last thing he'd wanted was to have her take fright at his very forthright mother's insistence on tradition and start backing away from the arrangement they had in place.

But even with all of this, it was now perfectly clear that there were parts of her that still bore a lasting resentment because of the way their relationship had originally started.

Why else would she be on the verge of tears and yet not want to tell him why?

'What do you mean by "in this instance"?' he demanded, striding towards the door and heading fast to the bank of lifts.

Most of his employees had already left. The hardcore workaholics barely glanced up as he headed down to the underground car park where his Ferrari was waiting.

'I have to go.'

'Tell me where. Unless it's some kind of big secret?'

'Goodness, Matias!' Hesitation on the other end of the phone. 'Okay, I'm heading to Charing Cross hospital.'

Matias froze by his car, sickened at the thought that something was wrong with her or the baby. 'I will meet you there.'

'No!'

He stilled, unwilling to deal with what her stricken response was saying to him. 'Okay...'

'Matias, I'll see you back at the house. Later. I don't know what time but I'll text or I'll try to. You know what they can be like at hospitals.'

'This is my baby as well, Sophie. I want to be by your side if there's any kind of problem.'

'There's no problem there. Don't worry.'

Naturally, Matias didn't believe her. Her voice was telling a different story. She was frantic with worry but when it came to the crunch, she didn't want him by her side to help her deal with it.

She would show up the following morning and would be bright and cheery and would downplay his concern and they would paper over the unsettling reality that in a time of crisis she would simply not allow him to be there for her.

There was no point driving to the hospital—the parking would be hellish—but Matias was going to be there. He was not going to let her endure anything she might find distressing on her own, and, he grimly acknowledged, it wasn't simply because it was a question of *their* child.

He didn't think twice. His driver was on standby. He would hit the hospital running before she even got there. Playing the long game was at an end. Like it or not, there was going to be a pivotal change in their relationship and if he had to force her hand, then so be it.

Rushing into the hospital after too many hold-ups and traffic jams to count, Sophie raced through the revolving doors and there he was, right in front of her.

He towered, a dark, brooding presence restlessly pacing, hand shoved deep in his trouser pocket. A billionaire out of his comfort zone and yet still managing to dominate his surroundings in a way that brought her to an immediate skidding halt. The cast of his beautiful face was forbidding. People were making sure not to get too close because he emanated all kinds of danger signals that made her tense up.

'Matias…'

Eyes off the entrance for five seconds, her voice brought him swinging round to look at her. 'I'm coming with you,' he said grimly. 'You're not going to push me out this time.'

'I haven't got time to do this right now,' but her heart was beating wildly as she began walking quickly towards the bank of lifts, weaving through the crowds.

'Sophie!' He stopped her, his hand on her arm, and she swung to face him. *'Talk to me.'*

Their eyes tangled and she sighed and said quietly, 'Okay. It's time we had a talk. It's time you knew...'

CHAPTER TEN

MATIAS EXPECTED HER to head straight to the maternity ward. However, she ignored the signs, moving fast towards the lift and punching a floor number while he kept damn close to her, willing her to talk and yet chilled by her remoteness. She barely seemed aware of his presence as she walked quickly up to one of the nurses at a desk and whispered something urgently to her, before, finally, turning around and registering that he was still there.

Matias looked at her carefully, eyes narrowed. They hadn't yet exchanged as much as a sentence. He was a guy who had always made it his duty to keep his finger on the pulse and know what was going on around him, because if you knew the lay of the land you were never in for unpleasant surprises, but right now he didn't have a clue what was going on and he hated that, just as he hated the distance between them.

Was this the point when everything began to fall apart? A sick chill filtered through his veins like poison.

'What's going on?' he asked tightly and Sophie sighed.

'You'll find out soon enough and then we'll need to talk.' She spun round and he followed as she walked straight towards one of the rooms to gently push open the door.

Matias had no idea what to expect and the last thing he was expecting to see was a young man on the bed, obviously sedated because his movements were sluggish as he turned in the direction of the door, but as soon as he saw Sophie he smiled with real love and tenderness.

Matias hovered in complete confusion. He felt like an intruder. He wasn't introduced. He was barely noticed by the man in the bed. He was there to watch, he realised, and so he did for the ten minutes she gently spoke to the boy, holding his hand, squeezing it and whispering in soft, soothing, barely audible tones.

She stroked his forehead and then kissed him before standing up and gazing down at the reclining figure. The boy had closed his eyes and was breathing evenly, already falling into sleep.

She glanced at Matias, nodded as she raised one finger to her lips, and only when they were outside the room did she turn to him.

'You're wondering,' she said without preamble. He was so shockingly beautiful and she loved him so much and yet Sophie felt as though they had now reached a turning point from which there would be no going back. She hadn't considered when the time would be *right* for him to meet Eric. Fear of an eventual negative outcome had held her back but Fate had taken matters into her own hand and now here they were.

'Can you blame me?' Matias responded tersely, raking his fingers through his hair, his whole body restless with unanswered questions.

'We need to talk but I don't think the hospital is quite the right place, Matias.'

Matias was gripped by that chill of apprehension again because there was something final in her voice. 'My place. It'll be quicker than trying to get back to the cottage.' On this one, single matter he could take charge and he did. Within ten minutes they were sitting in the back of his car, heading to his penthouse apartment, to which she had been only a handful of times.

The silence between them was killing him but he instinctively knew that the back seat of a car was not the place to start demanding answers any more than the environs of a hospital would have been.

He glanced at her a couple of times, at her averted profile, but she was mentally a million miles away and he found that incredibly frustrating. He wanted to reach out and yank her back to him. He found that he just couldn't bear the remoteness.

Caught up wondering how she was going to broach the taboo subject she had successfully managed to avoid so far, Sophie was barely aware of the car purring to a stop outside the magnificent Georgian building that housed his state-of-the-art modern penthouse apartment.

It was an eye-wateringly expensive place, now seldom used because he had become so accustomed to spending time at the cottage. They had fallen into a pattern of behaviour and it was only now, when the possibility of it disappearing was on the horizon, that she could really appreciate just how happy she had been.

Even though she knew that he didn't love her, he was perfect in so many ways. He just didn't feel about her the way she felt about him.

The cool, minimalist elegance of his apartment never failed to impress her, although, for her, it was a space she could never have happily lived in.

Now, though, with so much on her mind, she barely noticed the large abstract canvasses, the pale marble flooring, the pale furniture, the subtle, iconic sculptures dotted here and there.

She went directly to the cream leather sofa and sat down, immediately leaning forward in nervous silence and watching as he sat down opposite her, his body language mirroring hers.

'So?' Matias asked, his beautiful eyes shuttered and tension making his voice cooler than intended. 'Are you going to tell me who that guy was?' He saw the way she was struggling to find the right words and he added, tersely, 'An ex-boyfriend?'

'I beg your pardon?'

'Is he an ex-boyfriend, Sophie?' Matias demanded icily. 'The love of your life who may have been involved in an accident? I watched the interaction between the two of you. You love the guy.' Something inside him ripped. 'How long has he been disabled? Motorbike accident?' Every word was wrenched out of him but he had to know the truth.

'I do love him,' Sophie concurred truthfully. 'I've always loved him.'

Matias's jaw clenched as the knot in his stomach tightened. He wasn't going to lose it but he wanted to hit something hard.

'And he wasn't involved in an accident, at least not in the way you mean. Eric has been like that since he was born.'

Matias stilled, eyes keen, every pulse in his body frozen as he tried to grapple with what she was saying.

'Eric is my brother, Matias,' Sophie said quietly.

'Your brother...'

'He lives in a home just outside London, but something spooked him and he had a panic attack and went a little berserk. Hence why he's in hospital. He hurt himself while he was thrashing around. Nothing serious but they couldn't deal with it at the home.'

'You have a brother and you never told me...'

'I have no idea where to begin, Matias. If you just sit and listen, I'll try and make sense. My father only had contact with our family because he was left without a choice. When Eric was born, my mother knew that the only way she would ever be able to afford to take care of him would be with financial help from James. She had a lot of faults but a lack of devotion to Eric wasn't one of them. She made sure James paid for Eric's home, which is very expensive, and when she died it was up to me to make sure he carried on paying. It sounds callous, Matias, but it was the only way.'

'You wanted me to invest in your father's business because you wanted to make sure he could carry on paying for your brother's care.'

Sophie nodded, relieved but not terribly surprised that he had picked it up so quickly. For better or worse, it was a relief to be explaining this to him. If he chose to walk away, then so be it. She would be able to deal with the consequences, even though she knew that she would never be the same again without him in her life.

'I've always managed to put aside a nest egg and I've been dipping into it to cover the costs of Eric's home since James's business went to the wall, but, yes, I encouraged you to think that investing in James would be a good idea, not because I wanted the money for myself, but because I would have done anything, I'm afraid, to make sure my brother is safe and happy.'

'Why didn't you tell me?'

'How could I, Matias?' Sophie tilted her chin at a mutinous angle, defensive and challenging. 'You used me to confirm your suspicions about James and even when you came back into my life, it was because you felt you had no choice.'

'Sophie…'

'No, let me finish!' Her eyes glistened because if the end was coming then she would have to be strong and she didn't feel strong when she was here, looking at him and loving him with every bone in her body. 'I didn't tell you about Eric because there was no way I wanted you to think that you could exact more revenge by going public with what my father had done, shaming him by telling the world that he had fathered a disabled child he had never met and only supported because he had no choice.'

And just like that, Matias knew the depth of her distrust of him. Just like that he saw, in a blinding flash, how much he had hurt her. She had bowed her head and listened to him accuse her of things she had never been guilty of, and she had closed herself off to him. She clearly didn't trust him and she never would.

'I wish you had told me,' he said bleakly.

'How could I?' Sophie returned sadly. 'How could I take the risk that you might have been tempted to involve Eric in your revenge scheme, when the press would have turned it into a story that would have ended up hurting him, destroying both his privacy and his dignity? And also…'

Matias was processing everything she said, knowing that he had no one but himself and his blind drive for vengeance to blame for where he was right now. 'Also?' He looked at her.

'Eric is fragile. When Alan, my ex-boyfriend, walked out of my life, having met him just the once, Eric was heartbroken and felt responsible. I thought Alan was the one for me and I just didn't think that he would walk away because the duty of caretaking Eric was too much.'

'Any creep who would walk away from you because of that was never the one for you,' Matias grated harshly. 'You should count your lucky stars you didn't end up with him.'

'You're right. What I felt for Alan wasn't love. I liked him. I thought he was safe, and safe was good after my mother's experiences with men. But yes, I had a lucky escape. Don't think I don't know that.'

'I was driven by revenge.' Matias breathed in deeply and looked at her with utter gravity. 'It was always there, at the back of my mind. I was always going to be ambitious, I guess. I was always going to be fuelled to make money because I knew what it was like to have none, but I also knew what it was like to know that *I should have.* Your father was to blame and that became the mantra that energised a lot of my decisions. For a while, the chase for financial security became a goal in itself but then, like I told you, my mother fell ill and I discovered those letters. At the point when you entered my life, my desire to even the score with your father was at its height and…you became entangled in that desire. You didn't deserve it.'

Sophie looked at him questioningly, urging him to carry on and weak with relief that he seemed to have taken the situation with her brother in his stride.

'I thought you wanted to push me into investing into someone you knew was on the verge of bankruptcy and probably crooked as well because you wanted to carry on receiving an allowance from him.'

'I understand,' Sophie conceded, 'that you would have thought that because you knew nothing about Eric… You didn't know that there were other reasons for my doing what I did.'

'I saw red,' Matias admitted. 'I felt I'd been used and I reacted accordingly, but the truth was that deep down I knew you weren't that kind of person. *Querida*, you didn't trust me enough to tell me about your brother and I can't begin to tell you how gutted I am by that, even though I know that I have no one but myself to blame. I expected you to wipe away the past as though it had never existed, and I couldn't appreciate that I hurt you way too much for you to find that easy to do.'

This was the first time Matias had ever opened up and she knew from the halting progress of his words that it was something he found difficult, which made her love him even more. He was apologising and it took a big man to do that.

'I never want to hurt you again, my darling. And I will always make sure that your brother is protected and cared for in the way he deserves. Just give me the chance to prove to you how much I love you and how deeply sorry I am for putting you in the position of not thinking you could trust me with the most important secret in your life.'

Sophie's eyes widened and her heart stopped

beating before speeding up until she felt it burst through her ribcage.

'Did I just hear you say…?'

'I love you,' Matias told her simply. 'I never thought that I would fall in love. I was never interested in falling in love, but you came along and you got under my skin and before I knew it you had become an indispensable part of my life. When we went our separate ways, it was weird but I felt as though part of me had been ripped away. I didn't understand what that was about, but now I realise you were already beginning to occupy an important position in my life.'

'You never said,' Sophie breathed. 'Why didn't you say?'

'How could I?' Matias smiled wryly at her. He stood up and went to sit on the sofa next to her but he didn't try and pull her towards him, instead choosing to reach out and link her slender fingers through his. He absently played with her ring finger, giving no thought to what that said about the road his subconscious mind was travelling down. 'I was barely aware of it myself. We never expect the things that take us by surprise. Love took me by surprise.'

'As it did me,' Sophie confessed, so happy that she wanted to laugh and cry at the same time. 'When I first met you, I hated you.'

Matias's eyebrows shot up and he shot her a wolfish smile. 'Yet you still managed to find me incredibly sexy...'

'Don't be so egotistical, Matias.' But Sophie couldn't resist smiling back at him because he could be incredibly endearing in his puffed-up self-assurance. 'I thought I was going to see Art and instead I was shown into the lion's den.'

'It's a good job you *didn't* see Art,' Matias said drily. 'You would have walked all over him. He would probably have ended up giving *you* a new car and forgetting all about the damage you did to mine. You charmed the socks off him.'

Sophie blushed. 'We would never have met, though...'

'We would have,' Matias asserted. 'Our paths were destined to cross, even if you *did* hate me on sight.'

'Well, you *were* threatening to pull the plug on my business because I'd bumped into your car...'

Matias acknowledged that with a rueful tilt of his head. 'And so the rest is history. But,' he mused thoughtfully, 'I *should* have suspected that the ease with which I became accustomed to the notion of being a father was a pointer as to how I felt about you. If I hadn't been so completely crazy about you, I would have never slipped into marriage proposal mode so seamlessly.'

'And then I turned you down...'

'You did. Repeatedly. You have no idea how much I've wanted to prove to you that you could take a chance on me.'

'And you have no idea how much I've wanted to take that chance, but I was just too scared. I think, to start with, it really was because I was suspicious and unsure as to what you might do if you found out about Eric. My gut told me that I could trust you, despite all the water under the bridge, but my gut had lied once and I dug my heels in and refused to listen to it a second time. And then, later, I was scared to think about how you might react to Eric. Alan had been a dreadful learning curve for me. I'd been hurt and bewildered at the man he turned out to be and Eric had been terribly upset. He doesn't have the wherewithal to cope with upsets like that. Whatever happened, it was very important to me that he not become collateral damage. I could cope with that but he would never be able to.'

'I'm glad I met him,' Matias said seriously. 'Now can we stop talking? Although, there *is* one thing I still have to say...'

'What's that?' Sophie whispered, on cloud nine.

'Will you stop sitting on the fence and marry me?'

'Hmm...' Sophie laughed and pulled him towards her and kissed him long and hard, and then she brushed his nose with hers and grinned. 'Okay. And by that I mean...yes, yes, yes!'

A handful of months later, another trip had been made to the hospital. Sophie's labour had started at three in the morning and had moved quickly so that by the time they made it to the maternity ward baby Luciana had been just about ready to say hello to her doting and very much loved-up parents.

She had been born without fuss at a little after nine the following morning.

'She has your hair.' Sophie had smiled drowsily at Matias, who had been sitting next to her, cradling his seven-pound-eight-ounce, chubby, dark-haired baby daughter.

'And my eyes.' He had grinned and looked lovingly at the woman without whom life meant nothing. His life had gone from grey to Technicolor. Once upon a time, he had seen the accumulation of wealth and power as an end unto itself. He had thought that lessons learnt about love and the vulnerable places it took you were enough to put any sensible guy off the whole Happy Ever After scenario for good. He had sworn that a life controlled was the only life worth living. He'd been wrong. The only life worth living was a life with the woman he adored at his side.

'And let's hope that's where the similarities end,' Sophie had teased, still smiling. 'I don't need someone else in my life who looks bewildered at the prospect of boiling an egg.'

And now, with their beloved baby daughter nearly six months old, they were finally getting married.

Sophie gazed at her reflection in the mirror of the country hotel where she and her various friends, along with Matias's mother, had opted to stay the night.

Rose Rivero was back on her feet and, as she had confided in her daughter-in-law-to-be some time previously, with so much to live for that there was no question of her being ill again any time soon.

'You look stunning,' Julie said and Matias's mother nodded. The three of them were putting the final touches to Sophie's outfit, making sure that every small rosebud on her hairpiece was just right. 'You're having the fairy-tale wedding you've always longed for.'

Sophie laughed and thought back to the journey that had brought her to this point. 'It's not exactly been straightforward,' she murmured truthfully.

'I could have told you that my son is anything but straightforward,' Rose quipped. 'But you've calmed him down and grounded him in ways I could never have imagined possible.'

'You wouldn't say that if you could see him storming through the house looking for his car keys, which he seems to misplace every other day.' Sophie laughed and walked to the door, while the other two followed, to be met by the rest of the bridal party in the reception down-stairs, where cars were waiting to take them to the quaint church, perched on a hillside with a spectacular view of the sea beneath.

Never in her wildest dreams had she imagined a life as perfect as this.

She still had an interest in the catering firm and frequently went there to help out, but it was largely left to Julie and her three helpers, who now ran the profitable business with a tight rein. Their beautiful new premises had been up and running for some months and they were even thinking of expanding and opening a restaurant where they would be able to showcase their talent on a larger scale and to a wider audience.

James Carney had avoided the harsh punishment originally planned by a vengeful Matias, but life had changed considerably for him. With the company no longer in his hands, he had been paid off and dispatched down to Cornwall where he would be able to lead a relatively quiet life, without the trappings of glamour that had been gained from his underhand dealings with Tomas Rivero. Occasionally he dropped Sophie an email and occasionally she answered, but she had no affection for the man who had made her mother's life and her own a nightmare of having to beg for handouts and always with the threat that those handouts could stop at any given moment.

Matias was in possession of the company, which his father should have jointly owned, and it was now a thriving concern, another strand in his hugely successful empire.

But it was with Eric where Sophie felt the greatest flush of pleasure, for her brother could not have been made more welcome by Matias and he was developing skills that still continued to amaze her. He was no longer living in his own little world, really only able to communicate with her, his carers and a handful of other patients. Now, he was making strides in communicating with the outside world, without the fear and panic that had previously dogged him, and she could only think that Matias's patience and little innocent Luciana were partly responsible for that progress. And maybe, she occasionally thought, he was intuitive enough to realise that the sister who came to visit him was no longer stressed out. He was safe for ever. He had begun a specially adapted computer course and was showing all sorts of talents hitherto untapped.

Sophie thought of her daughter as she was driven to the church. Luciana would be there, with her nanny, and although the ceremony would mean nothing to her she would enjoy the photos when she got older.

Sophie breathed in deeply as she stepped out of the chauffeur-driven Bentley and then she was in the church, as nervous as a kitten to be marrying the man who meant everything to her.

Matias turned as everyone did, as the music began to play. This was the final piece of the jigsaw. He was marrying the woman he loved and he could not have been prouder.

The breath hitched in his throat as he looked at her walk slowly up the aisle towards him. The cream dress fitted her body like a glove. She had returned to her former weight and all those luscious curves were back, tempting him every single time he looked at her. She was holding a modest bouquet of pale pink flowers and her veil was secured by a tiara of rosebuds that mimicked the flowers in her hand.

She was radiant. She was his. Possessiveness flared inside him, warming him.

He'd never contemplated marriage but now he knew he wouldn't have been complete without it, without her having his ring on her finger. And the wedding could not have been more to his taste. He might be a billionaire, but this simple affair was perfect.

'You look stunning, *querida*,' he murmured, when she was finally standing beside him and before they both turned to the priest.

'So do you.' Sophie gazed up at Matias. He did this to her, even though she saw him daily, even though he was as much a part of her life as the air she breathed. He made her breathing ragged and he made her heart skip a beat.

The special girl in my life, Matias thought with a swell of pride. Well…one of them.

He looked to the back of the church and there was the other one, being cradled by the nanny, fast asleep.

Matias smiled and knew that this was exactly where he was meant to be, and much later, when all the revelry had died down and the last of the guests had departed, he felt it again, that flare of hot possession as he gazed at the woman who was now his wife.

The following morning, they would be off on their honeymoon. Luciana would be there, as would her nanny and his mother.

'Why are you grinning?' Sophie asked, reaching to undo the pearl buttons of the lavender dress she had slipped into after the wedding ceremony had finished.

Sprawled on the four-poster bed in the hotel where they would be spending the night before flying by private jet to one of Matias's villas in Italy, he was a vision of magnificent male splendour. He had undone the buttons of his white shirt and it hung open, exposing a sliver of bronzed, hard chest.

'I'm grinning,' he drawled, 'because not many newly-weds take the groom's mother with them on their honeymoon.' He beckoned her to him with a lazy curl of his finger and watched, incredibly turned on, as she sashayed towards him, ridding herself of her clothes as she got nearer to his prone figure.

By the time she was standing next to the bed, she was wearing only the lacy bra that worked hard to contain her generous breasts and the matching, peach-coloured lacy pants.

Whatever he had to say to her flew through the window because he couldn't resist rolling to his side and then sliding his finger under the lacy pants so that he could press his face against her musky, honeyed wetness, flicking an exploring tongue along the crease of her womanhood and settling to enjoy her for a few moments as she opened her legs a fraction to allow his tongue entry.

Then he lay back and sighed with pure pleasure when, naked, she lay next to him and slipped her hand under his shirt.

'You and Luciana mean the world to her,' Matias said softly, 'and I want to thank you for that, for taking the sadness out of my mother's life and…' he stroked her hair and kissed her gently on her full mouth '… I want to thank you for being my wife. You put the sound and colour into my world and I would be nothing without you.'

Sophie pushed aside his shirt and licked his flat brown nipple until he was groaning and urging her down as he unzipped his trousers.

'I love you so much,' she whispered. 'Now you're going to have to keep quiet, husband of mine, because it's our honeymoon and there are a lot of things I want to do with you before the night is over…'

* * * * *

LET'S TALK

Romance

For exclusive extracts, competitions
and special offers, find us online:

f facebook.com/millsandboon

◎ @millsandboonuk

🐦 @millsandboon

Or get in touch on 0844 844 1351*

For all the latest titles coming soon,
visit millsandboon.co.uk/nextmonth

Want even more
ROMANCE?

Join our bookclub today!

'Mills & Boon books, the perfect way to escape for an hour or so.'

Miss W. Dyer

'Excellent service, promptly delivered and very good subscription choices.'

Miss A. Pearson

'You get fantastic special offers and the chance to get books before they hit the shops'

Mrs V. Hall

Visit millsandbook.co.uk/Bookclub and save on brand new books.

MILLS & BOON